MICHAE[...] wall and e[...] fore taking [...] government service, during which he [...] over the world as a diplomat, served as director of a United Nations agency and worked in counter-terrorism. With this experience he writes of the secret worlds of espionage and counter-espionage with insight and great authenticity. His first novel *Down Among The Dead Men* (1983) won him an international reputation – like *Seven Steps to Treason* (1985) and *The Third Betrayal* it was reviewed enthusiastically on both sides of the Atlantic and translated into many European languages and Japanese. His fourth thriller, which continues to follow the fortunes of spymaster David Nairn, will be published in 1988.

Michael Hartland is married with two daughters and lives in Devon.

'Skilful pattern of kidnap, blackmail, double and quadruple crossing . . . a taut tale of treachery.'
Punch

'Hartland paints an intriguing portrait and creates convincing characters whose fate will hold readers spellbound . . . A nail-biting tale: it all rings true'
Publishers Weekly

'There is a test for a good spy story – is the plot credible and are the characters real people? Michael Hartland's THE THIRD BE-TRAYAL gets full marks on both counts. If somebody told me that it was all true, I would believe it.'

Ted Allbeury

Also by Michael Hartland in Sphere Books:

DOWN AMONG THE DEAD MEN
SEVEN STEPS TO TREASON

The Third Betrayal

MICHAEL HARTLAND

SPHERE BOOKS LIMITED

Sphere Books Limited
27 Wrights Lane, London W8 5TZ
First published in Great Britain by
Hodder & Stoughton Limited, 1986
Copyright © Michael Hartland 1986
Published by Sphere Books 1987

TRADE
MARK

Set in 9½/10½pt Linotron Times by
Rowland Phototypesetting Limited
Bury St Edmunds, Suffolk

Printed and bound in Great Britain by
Cox and Wyman Limited, Reading, Berks

To two Soviet master spies,
whose political persuasion is not shared by the author,
but whose courage and skill admit only of admiration:

RICHARD SORGE

Executed in Sugamo Prison, Tokyo,
7 November, 1944
Hero of the Soviet Union

and

RUTH KUCZYNSKI

Order of the Red Banner 1937 & 1969

ACKNOWLEDGMENTS

The author is lastingly grateful to all who proffered assistance when he was researching this novel. In addition to those who have asked to remain anonymous, he offers warm thanks to Diana Davenport; Marilyn Phillips; Helen Webb, Librarian of the Athenaeum Club, London; Nigel West; and the staff of the University of Exeter Library.

'For the female of the species
is more deadly than the male.'

Rudyard Kipling
1865–1936

PROLOGUE

Somerset – 1973

His coffin was carried from the church and the congregation followed, silent and awkward, shuffling over the flagstones into the porch. Two men brought up the rear, one tall and gaunt. He gestured towards the wooden stocks preserved just outside the door and whispered to his companion: 'God, it's so bloody English. *Was* he a spy?'

'He was the head of MI5.'

'The two roles are not necessarily incompatible.' The words were spoken in a dry Scots accent and the speaker blinked as he emerged into the light. Above his head the yellow sandstone of the tower glowed in October sun, but a cold wind was slicing across the Somerset levels; he huddled into his shabby black overcoat. The coffin was being slid into a hearse.

'Going to the crematorium, David?'

'No, best leave that to his family and friends.'

The shorter man looked at him questioningly. 'Did he *have* any friends? Except in Moscow?' They stepped from the path and walked among the gravestones. The hearse was driving away followed by a procession of shiny black cars. 'And we even gave the bastard a knighthood – Christ, they must be laughing all the way to the Lubyanka.'

'There's no proof he was a Soviet agent. You and I have just wasted three years trying to nail him and getting nowhere. We'll never crack it now – he died at just the wrong time.'

'Or was it the right time? I mean, he was *in* the coffin?'

His companion laughed. 'Ay – we had a look at the undertakers. He was in that box all right.'

'What happens now?'

1

'Tomorrow we write a final report for the committee. Then I report back to the Cut for a posting. After this cock-up they'll probably send me to Angola. Will you go back to Curzon Street?'

'I suppose so.' He sighed. 'Did you see Fell in church?'

'No. He's lived as a recluse ever since he left the service.' The hollow face creased into a frown. 'Anyway, he'd hardly come to the funeral – Carteret crucified him. He must hate his guts.'

The other man turned and stared out across the barren marshland outside the churchyard. 'It can't rest there, David – we *must* have an answer. How can the service ever be trusted again until we do?'

'Your service, Jim, not mine . . .' They had reached a dark blue Ford Cortina and a uniformed driver held the back door open. He looked at the gaunt man questioningly. 'Where to, Mr Nairn?'

'Take the road to Bridgwater, please, and if Mr Simon agrees look for a decent pub.' The shorter man nodded consent with a smile.

As the car drove away, the young reporter from the local paper shifted on the church wall. Despite a thick overcoat he was getting cold. Snapping his notebook shut he eyed the girl perched on a tomb in a predatory fashion. She must be a journalist too, but where from? Odd. But what a bore. Sir Jack Carteret – some sort of dreary civil servant who'd been on the local council after he retired. He was fed up with funerals and half the people at this one had refused to give their names. It was hardly worth covering anyway.

2

PART ONE

Island of Pelicans

1

Island of Pelicans

The island loomed out of the mist, a jagged rock in the middle of the bay. Black cliffs rose to a plateau, weeping with rain, where watch-towers and wire fencing surrounded the flat block of the prison. At their foot, white-flecked seas smashed on the shore and swirled out to meet the Pacific.

The ferry bumped alongside the rotting piles of a landing stage. Diesel engines throttled back, two men in fatigues caught the mooring ropes and a dejected file descended the gangplank. They huddled together, slithering on the wet surface. Apart from the crash of waves, there was no sound as a uniformed figure approached and eyed the arrivals grimly.

'Welcome to the Rock.' The figure was a burly woman who clutched a parka around her and roared at them against the wind. 'I'm Debbie, your guide from the National Parks Service, Golden Gate recreation area.'

Sleet fell harder and the tall man at the back of the group turned up his overcoat collar. He was not much more than forty but his hair was already a distinguished grey and he had an air of confident gravity. Somewhere in the world, this man was important. He glanced at the other tourists, half hoping that his contact would not be among them. He had taken no serious risk so far, just a quick call from a payphone on Market Street to the FBI office, but soon it would be too late to turn back.

'So you're East German? But you want to come over to us?' The clipped Ivy League accent crackling over the phone had showed no emotion, neither welcoming nor suspicious. 'Don't come here. Can you be on Fisherman's Wharf in two hours? Take the eleven o'clock boat to Alcatraz.' The voice had chuckled. 'Alcatraz – somewhere to remind you of home. Of course the jail's closed now – it's a kind of museum. To identify yourself, carry a copy of the *Examiner* under your left arm. One of my colleagues will meet with you.'

The group of twenty had moved to shelter in the lee of the island, below a rusty sign:

UNITED STATES PENITENTIARY
Only Government boats permitted
Others must keep off 200 yards

They started to walk up the steep path to the cell-block, past derelict buildings and sagging wire fences. A bulbous water-tower rose in the mist ahead of them. The East German hung back and a middle-aged man fell in beside him. He wore a dark green windcheater over a business suit, with a tartan cap, and the German felt a flash of irritation. He had taken precautions not to be followed – joining the ferry at the last minute, barely seconds before it sailed – but this idiot looked exactly like an FBI man masquerading as a tourist.

'The Spaniards called it the Island of Pelicans,' said the American, looking straight ahead. 'I'm O'Brien.' Whatever his name was, it wasn't O'Brien. 'You the kraut who called the bureau?'

The German flushed at the casual insult. 'I am.'

'What's your name?'

'Peter.'

'Peter what, for Chrissake?'

'Peter Werner.'

'Is that *Doctor* Peter Werner?'

'It is.'

The American grunted, as if something had fallen into place. 'And you say you're an East German scientist? Over here for a conference?'

'Yes, I am.'

'What's your field?'

'Nuclear physics. I work at an institute attached to Humboldt University in East Berlin.'

The man looked at him thoughtfully, but with a hint of contempt. 'And now you want to stay in the nice cosy West? Make bombs for us instead of the commies?'

'I am not a weapons specialist, but yes, I do want to stay.'

'How many of you are there, from East Germany, at this conference?'

'Two. We always go in pairs.'

'Yeah, pal – that figures.'

They had reached the plateau, leaning into a bitter wind which swept across the patch of concrete between the jail and the white tower of a lighthouse. Through a gash in the mist they could see the skyscrapers of the city and the spidery red outline of the bridge across the Golden Gate. A foghorn croaked out in the bay.

'You got a family, Peter?'

'No. I am divorced.'

'That makes it easier. When you due back in Berlin?'

'In five days. I have permission to stop for a couple of nights in Brussels – I shall visit a friend who is living there for a year with her husband. He is in our trade mission.'

'So you want to defect in Brussels?'

'That is correct, but then I wish to live in America. My friend wishes to leave her husband and come too, with her family.'

'Her *family*?'

'She has two children.'

The American snorted. 'Jesus Christ – and anyone else?' The other tourists were entering the door of the derelict cell-block. 'Lot of people ask for asylum, Peter, but not by the friggin' bus-load. Could take a little time to arrange.' He paused questioningly. 'You got anything special to offer, if you ain't in weapons? Espionage? Security work?' He raised his eyebrows and laughed.

'I said I am a scientist. But yes, I *do* have something else to offer – something your CIA and British intelligence would give their right arms for.'

'Yeah?' He looked sceptical. The rain had stopped and the woman who was their guide was waving from the doorway, calling them to hurry up. A patch of wintry sun lit the

7

cracked front of the building, with its two rows of barred windows and an American eagle squatting on the Federal coat of arms above the door.

The German seized the other man's arm urgently. 'Help me – for God's sake *help me*.' His voice rose. 'I promise I can give you information on penetration at the very top of British counter-intelligence – information of real value to your government.'

The American ignored the guide and stared, still sceptically, into the frightened eyes of the German. 'Tell me more, buddy.'

'I also have information about the Soviet agent – a very powerful and high-ranking Soviet agent – who was responsible for this penetration.'

The American yawned as if he had heard it all before. 'If that's your story it had better be true, Peter. Where can I call you this evening?'

'But are you going to help me?' He was almost shouting. 'I want to *defect*. I have placed myself in great danger by talking to you.'

Suddenly the FBI man grinned reassuringly. 'If you're genuine we'll help you, we always do. Sorry if I seemed off-hand – we're just a little cautious. I'll make a report to Washington and have an answer for you this evening. It may not be a final answer. Where can I call you?'

'You cannot "call" me,' snapped the German, his fear suddenly giving way to anger. 'I have to share a hotel room with my colleague – for security reasons. Don't you know that? Give me a number where I can telephone *you*.'

'All rightey.' He fumbled in a pocket, pulled out an empty cigarette pack and scribbled a number on it. 'Call after eight.'

The German tore the packet in half and wrote something; he thrust it back at the FBI man. 'I have written the code-name of the Soviet agent on this. Be sure to give that name to your headquarters in Washington. It will mean much to them.'

The other man shrugged and grinned again. 'Sure. Sure – I'll do that. Just call me this evening.' He turned away and hurried down the path, slithering on the loose gravel.

2

London

Sir James Simon stood up and smiled broadly as Nairn came in. 'David – thanks for coming over. It's good to see you looking so well again. Must be the monkey glands.'

'It was a heart bypass operation, but it seems to have worked.' The dry Scots speech had not changed, nor had his gaunt appearance. Nairn settled into one of the leather armchairs and looked around while Simon poured two glasses of sherry. It was a room with walls emulsioned a dirty cream – not panelled like those at the back of the Cabinet Office – but there was a fine antique desk and conference table, as befitted the co-ordinator of the intelligence services, the man to whom the heads of MI5 and MI6 deferred, or were supposed to defer. Simon had done pretty well, Nairn thought without rancour, despite their joint failure that had ended in a Somerset churchyard thirteen years ago. All the same, that desk – and the sherry – were too good to be official issue and must be his own. The windows gave on to Whitehall, where several thousand demonstrators against Cruise missiles were chanting and jeering at the police as they barred the entrance to Downing Street.

'How long have you been back at work, David?'

'About six months.'

'And you really are fit now? Not still planning to retire early?'

'I never was – it was Walker who wanted me to go.'

'Yes, I suppose it was.' Simon smiled and Nairn met his soft brown eyes. They hid great wisdom and the worldly experience of a little boy born in the Ottakringer district of Vienna in 1927, destined to be orphaned in a concentration

9

camp and arrive penniless at Southampton in 1946. Now he was so very, very British. 'I'm staying in town tonight,' he said. 'Rachel is going to the WI. Would you like to have dinner with me at the Athenaeum?'

'Gladly.' Nairn lived alone in a squalid flat in Chiswick. 'I suppose you want to talk about something?'

'Of course, but first there are some things we can't discuss outside this office.' He stood up and closed a sash window, as if the roaring mob outside might somehow overhear. 'I'm going to be indiscreet – you won't let me down?'

Nairn shook his head and smiled inwardly. They had worked together, on and off, for over twenty years, but he was still amused when his old friend became dramatic and conspiratorial, as if consciously aping a character from C. P. Snow's *Corridors of Power*.

'The PM is considering who should run the Security Service when Alexander retires in a few months time.'

'I thought the deputy normally took over?'

'Not this time, old friend, she's had enough. Five needs sorting out. It's been a shambles for too long. In my time they were all suffering from paranoia, looking at their navels, trying to cover up the Carteret scandal. They're supposed to be catching spies, keeping an eye on Soviet agents infiltrating that lot.' He jerked a thumb towards the window. 'Not buggering about chasing each other's tails. My God – it's got to the point where the IRA can blow up half the Cabinet in Brighton, without being sussed beforehand and without being caught afterwards.'

'That bomb was hardly Five's fault.'

'Wasn't it? Why the hell not?' With his flashing eyes, hooked nose and mane of silver hair, Simon looked exactly like the Levantine merchants his ancestors must have been. 'Their job is to preserve the security of the realm. Instead they've been impotent for years. Penetrated by Moscow, but never able to find the traitors and cut the canker out. Was Carteret really a traitor twenty years ago and who did he leave behind? Who's the traitor *now*? Eh? Why does the whole set-up produce failure after failure, year after year?'

'Maybe it *is* penetrated, but I've never been quite convinced. It could just be that their morale is so destroyed after all these years of internal witch hunts, that the place doesn't work effectively any more.'

'But David, dear boy, this is our national *Security Service*. The fabled MI5. It *must* be effective. The enemy aren't coming in tanks these days, they're coming up through the bloody floor.'

'You said the PM was appointing a new DG. Who?'

'Ah, yes, the new head of MI5. Well, there are several names, and I'm not supposed to tell you this, David, but top of her little list is someone we both know pretty well.'

'You, Jim?'

Simon shook his head. 'No, not me.' He gave a theatrical gesture and beamed like a conjuror producing a rabbit from a hat. 'As a matter of fact it's you, *mon vieux*.'

Nairn showed no reaction. Simon's histrionics always made him behave more dourly than was really in his nature. Eventually he drained his glass. 'How curious. I've never been in Five in my life. I don't know the half of what they do . . . they'd resent an outsider bitterly . . . and I don't want that kind of responsibility any more, I'll be sixty in a couple of years. She's finally gone round the bend.'

'Actually it was my idea.'

'Then you're barmy.'

'Not at all. She wants someone good – and someone she can trust. Just for a few years, to get the place back on the rails. You'll do it, David, you know you will.'

'Will I?'

'You will if she asks you. You don't want to retire, do you? What would you find to do all day, down there by the river in Chiswick? Of course,' he shuffled the papers in his lap, 'there's no decision yet. There are other names . . . and some difficulties to be sorted out. We shan't know the outcome for a while. But I thought you should know. Now you'd better forget I ever told you.'

'Of course.'

Simon stood up and poured more sherry. 'There's something else I'd like to discuss.'

Nairn looked at him warily. 'I don't trust you when you come bearing gifts, Jim. I don't think I want to hear any more.'

11

'It's about Carteret . . . the Sanctuary Committee.'

'Oh God, no,' Nairn began to laugh. 'Not after all this time. I had enough of all that long ago – surely the committee was wound up after Carteret died?'

'It hasn't *met*, but it still exists. The case was never closed, because we could never reach a conclusion. Did you know that Fell is still visited every month? He's been offered immunity from prosecution if he confesses.'

'Good grief – d'you mean they've been hounding the poor bastard for twenty years? It's inhuman. He was perfectly innocent – Carteret just used him as a decoy.'

Simon shrugged. 'Sad necessity. Unfortunately Carteret is dead but Fell alive – I promise you it is all done most discreetly. But that is not what I want to discuss.' Silently he handed over a telegram, which Nairn read slowly.

'Is this straight up?' Nairn's dour expression had suddenly given way to animation, the light of battle in his eyes. 'A defector who can finger Sonia? After all this time and misery – we might actually be able to crack it? My God.'

'Exactly, dear boy. The man claims to be her son, no less. We might finally be on to the answer, just in time for you to take over and clean the stables. Let's walk round to the club.' He stood up and put the papers from his desk into an open safe. 'By the way,' he glanced over his shoulder, 'I want you to take it on, independently of both Five and Six. And I want you to meet this fellow. In Belgium. Tomorrow.' He closed the thick steel door and spun the combination dial until the lock clicked.

'Okay – I imagine there are plenty of flights.'

'My secretary has already booked two seats to Brussels at 10.05. I imagine you'll take someone to watch your back?'

'Don't waste time, do you, Jim? And exactly what am I supposed to tell this fellow when I meet him?'

PART TWO

1930–1946

3

Shanghai – 1930

One of the severed heads was still bleeding. It was impaled on a pole, down which a trickle of blood dripped slowly into the yellow earth. The contorted face, eyes open and staring in terror, was that of a young woman with long black hair, about Ruth's own age. A few feet away the two bodies lay covered in flies. The Chinese characters scrawled on a placard proclaimed that they were Communist bandits.

Ruth wanted to retch, but clutched her shopping bag and managed to keep her head high as she pushed through the bustling Chinese crowd. If you were confused, faint in the heat and close to tears, the best thing was to look like a European. A rickshaw coolie was squatting between his shafts at the street corner. Against all her principles she sank into the cushioned seat and asked for the international settlement, trying to forget the hideous masks of death. The elderly man picked up the shafts. He wore only a pair of blue shorts, below which his bony legs, knotted with taut muscle, started to trot along the cobbles.

Half an hour later Ruth was sitting on the shaded verandah of the small brick house, with its distant view to the sky-scrapers by the river. The banyan trees waved in the breeze that always carried a strong smell of burnt sugar from the port. She sipped a bowl of green tea and tried to put her thoughts in order. Two different worlds, just a rickshaw ride from each other, and she did not belong properly to either of them. For six months she had lived in the comfort of this European compound, playing tennis with other bored wives by day and dining with Rolf at the club in the evening. An upper-class Jewish girl from Berlin, now married to a respectable architect furthering his career by working for

15

the Shanghai city council. Yet only miles away a whole vast country was disintegrating with war and revolution. The civil war between Communists and Kuomintang had been raging across China for three years. Shanghai was a Nationalist city, but they executed so many Communists that there must be a strong underground.

Ruth lay back in the rocking chair and languidly stretched her legs. They were long and slender and the bones in her ankles cracked. The hot, moist air was making her drowsy – but she was no longer in any doubt which world was for her. In her heart she had known for at least ten years.

She woke with a start. It was dusk and for a few seconds her vision remained blurred. Then she saw him – a man of medium height in a Panama hat and white linen suit. He smiled up at her from below the verandah: he had a strong, Slavic face, thick black hair and penetrating eyes. She stood up slowly, not knowing what to do.

'May I come up?' he asked in German.

'Of course, but who are you? What do you want?' she faltered. 'My husband will be home soon.'

'I know.' It was an odd, unsettling reply. He climbed the steps and followed her into the empty living room. In the light she could see that the eyes above his high cheekbones were humorous as well as piercing; and he was quite incredibly handsome. She pushed away the foolish stirring in her body and became a bustling German *Hausfrau*. 'Would you like a drink?'

'Thank you – perhaps some beer?'

They sat in the creaking basket chairs and it was Ruth who broke the awkward silence. 'Who are you?' she asked again. 'What do you want?'

He smiled. 'We have a mutual friend, Agnes Smedley. Didn't she tell you to expect me?'

She started. 'Agnes? No.'

'I have known Agnes for some time. She thought you might be able to help me.'

'But who *are* you?'

'At this stage it does not matter who I am.'

She flushed at the correction. 'Then how should I help

you?' Her voice was level despite her inner confusion. He looked at her searchingly and she sat very upright, knees demurely together.

'You are Ruth Kuczynski.' It was a statement, not a question.

'I am Frau Ursula Friedmann.'

'But you were born Kuczynski, in Berlin, twenty-four years ago – and you prefer to be called Ruth.' She shifted uncomfortably. 'And you joined the Communist Youth League when you were seventeen.'

'Yes, my father brought up all his children as Marxists – but we took our own decisions to join the Party.'

He nodded. 'I know.'

'But *how* do you know so much about me?' Like the animal power he radiated, it was disturbing, almost frightening.

'There is no time to explain now – your husband will, indeed, be back soon. Agnes tells me that you are ready to become more active and I have been observing you for some time.' She flushed again. 'I think you really *were* expecting me?'

'Was I?' The notion of being 'observed' made her begin to feel angry rather than threatened.

'I too am German. I am a comrade – and I need help.' His eyes met hers abruptly. 'Will you work with me, Ruth?'

'Work with you? I'm sorry,' she spoke slowly. 'I really don't understand what you mean.'

'You have placed yourself under the discipline of the Party – you know perfectly well what I mean.'

She felt a surge of excitement mingled with fear. This was different from meetings in dusty rooms above Berlin cafés; this was *real*. She still did not know his name – and knew better than to ask again – but she felt it natural for him to be there, so confident and commanding. Then she pictured the two beheaded Chinese and hesitated, but he was already standing up. 'May I come to see you again tomorrow -- at ten in the morning?'

Her head spun again. 'Yes.' She had only half taken the decision and it was as if someone else were speaking. 'Yes – ten would be convenient.'

4

Shanghai – 1931

The motor-cycle shot off down the dirt road, then slowed and made a tight turn a quarter of a mile away. It wobbled dangerously, but the rider kept balance and returned in a nearly straight line, stopping in a flurry of gravel, arms straight to the controls and feet outstretched to the ground to keep the bike upright.

He sprang from the shade of the pine trees with a shout of laughter. 'Bravo, Ruth – well done! Were you terrified?'

She grinned back at him. 'No. Well – just a little, at first.' He held the motor-cycle while she jumped off, then they both remounted, with Ruth riding pillion. He revved the spluttering engine and roared off up the valley, flashing through alternate patches of dazzling sunlight and dark shade where banyan trees met over the road.

It was over a year since they had first met. After that first encounter he had returned and asked her to deliver a package for him under cover of night, to a house in the Chinese quarter. She knew it was a test and had spent the afternoon in a state of terror, counting the dangers: assault and robbery, rape, arrest by the blueshirts as a foreign agent, torture, execution. Eventually she had started to laugh at herself, dressed in trousers to look more like a Chinese in the dark, and pedalled off on her bicycle. Once her fear had gone, it had been strangely exhilarating – and she was back, triumphant, in less than an hour.

After that there were more tests; and it had been a month or more before he told her his name – Richard Sorge – and that they were both working for the Fourth Bureau of the Red Army. It seemed quite natural, almost as if some higher force had brought her to China for that very purpose. Within

18

two months Richard was secretly meeting Chinese comrades and visitors from Moscow in an upper room at her house while Rolf was at work. Within three months they had become lovers and now she often lay beside Rolf at night, eyes open in the dark, cherishing her secret happiness – for suddenly, at the age of twenty-four, Ruth Kuczynski had discovered the two great commitments that were to rule her life.

After half an hour they stopped in a small hamlet, which Sorge said was called Ming-on. Outside a long wooden building, with a curving roof of red pantiles, six women squatted at low tables, working like automatons. Their faces were expressionless, eyes sunk into gaunt skulls, ragged sleeves thrown back to reveal bony arms ugly with knotted muscle. Their fingers moved so fast that it was impossible to see what they were doing, except that it involved knives and wood. An overseer stood by, flourishing a long rattan.

'They are making matches,' explained Sorge softly. 'One thousand a day avoids a whipping.'

'How much are they paid?'

'The equivalent of fifteen pfennigs, for about fourteen hours work.'

'But that's nothing – it's barbaric!'

Sorge nodded. 'Quite. And, although they look old, they are all young girls of less than twenty, some only children. That is one reason why the Party has such strong support in Shanghai.' They walked along the dusty street until they came to a tea-house, a low ramshackle building where coolies dressed only in vests and blue shorts squatted on stools with bowls of tea. A few were also devouring rice – bowl in one hand, clicking chopsticks in the other – with hurried jerky movements as if it might be the last food on earth.

The Chinese eyed the European couple curiously. Hand in hand they jumped over the open drain, running with thick brown water, and she laughingly wrinkled her nose at the stench. They sat in the shade, a handsome pair. He had strong features and an air of authority. Her face was cheerful, more round than oval, with a broad smile and mop of short, wavy, black hair. In contrast her body was slim and delicate. As the waiter brought them bowls of tea and a tin plate of nuts, she crossed her knees and the blue cotton of her skirt slipped back to reveal long, elegant legs, burnt brown by the Chinese sun. Her movements were almost oriental, languid and sensual.

'Did you read the IG-Farben paper and my report?' he asked.

'I read *everything* you give me, Richard, often in bed at night when Rolf is out. My bed is my university.'

Sorge roared with laughter and she blushed, then eyed him provocatively, but suddenly his face became severe. 'It is important to keep up your reading. One day you will be on your own and the Centre will give you great responsibility.'

She started and he smiled, leaning forward to stroke her thigh. 'Someone has just walked over your grave?'

Gently she removed his hand and glanced meaningfully at the watching Chinese, her eyes troubled. 'I can't bear the thought of us being separated; every time you touch me I tell myself it is for ever.' She looked away wistfully. 'That Russian proverb is so true – where my love is, there is my life.'

'But we are in an army, Ruth – soon the Centre will send you in one direction and me in the other. And we shall obey.'

'Then we must be together again when we are old, too old to fight any more . . . in Moscow, or in a socialist Germany.'

'That would be good.' He sounded awkward and was about to add something when the air was rent by high-pitched screams and a flurry of shouting. They stood up as coolies ran from the tea-house and figures appeared from the huts: old men and women, mothers clutching children. Two men were dragging a girl into the middle of the street.

'There must be an industrial dispute at the match factory.' Sorge gripped Ruth's arm urgently. 'Whatever you feel, you can do nothing to help. For God's sake, keep quiet and learn.'

The girl was still screaming in terror as she was flung face down in the dust. One man knelt and pinioned her arms while the other drew off her black trousers. She kicked wildly, but he seized her ankles as the growing crowd gaped at her naked thighs and bowed legs. A third man in a long patterned gown and round skull-cap threw a strip of wet cheesecloth across the cringing buttocks. He stepped back and raised his rattan high in the air. The crowd fell silent.

'A woman may not be shamefully exposed,' whispered Sorge, 'except on the execution ground.'

The long cane whistled through the air and whipped viciously across the girl's hips. The sudden shock stopped her screams and a line of blood appeared on the wet cloth. The crowd murmured. As the rattan fell again the victim gave a shriek which faded into a choked whimper. Ruth winced and clung to Sorge. 'It's so *cruel*, Richard. Can't we do anything to stop them?'

He drew her away and they hurried back to the motor-cycle. 'I wish to God we could. Keep quiet or they'll treat you the same way. I'm sorry – this is no place for Europeans.' The crack of the blows pursued them down the street, now punctuated by hideous animal cries of pain.

They breasted a low hill outside Shanghai early in the evening. The great city lay silently beside the muddy curve of the Whangpoo, a dying sun bathing the skyscrapers along the Bund in crimson. Sorge stopped and put the bike on its stand. They were in the shadow of some trees and he felt for Ruth's body. 'Is Rolf still away in Peking?'

Her eyes flashed up at him, white in the darkness. 'Yes, you may stay the night. The amah is used to it.' She took his hand and pulled it away, but continued to hold it firmly. 'Later, darling. I can't get that poor girl out of my mind.'

He nodded gently. 'I understand. Then we will use this moment to talk a little business – Sonia.' She smiled at his use of the code-name the Centre had given her a few months before. 'There is an Englishman here in Shanghai, who works now for a tobacco company, but started as a journalist. He might possibly be useful to us and I want to find out all about him. Get to know him personally if you can.'

'Why me?'

'Because he uses the international club like you and Rolf and I suspect he also lives in the settlement.'

21

'And what is he called?'

'Carteret. Jack Carteret. See what you can do – it may come to nothing,' he shrugged, 'but who knows . . .'

There was a strange rumbling sound in the air and they both turned towards the city. 'My God,' cried Sorge. 'It's an air raid. The Japanese must be further south than we thought.' Ruth stared and huddled into his shoulder. A small group of aircraft was banking in the dark sky and they could hear the distant thud of explosions. Within seconds a line of yellow flame slashed across the city, lighting up the jagged skyline until it vanished behind clouds of oily black smoke. The Imperial Japanese army had invaded Manchuria six months before. Now they were sweeping south, efficient and brutal, crushing a poor and divided people. Until this evening Shanghai had been spared.

5

Shanghai – 1932

Ruth wished that she could stop trembling. She smiled down at the baby and rocked his wooden crib, clinging to normality. Michael – Micha – would be a year old in February, just two weeks away. Outside, the city was in turmoil. Chiang's blueshirts still roamed the streets shooting suspected Communists, even with the threat of the Japanese war machine only miles away; food was short and every morning beggars lay dead in the streets.

Through the window she could see yet another air raid. The Japanese bombers were so far away that she could barely hear the screaming metal as they dived, or the thuds of explosions which followed: it was like a silent film. But that morning she had seen the splintered ruins and the piles of rotting corpses. Riding her bicycle, she had been turned back by Nationalist troops near Chapei, because half a mile further into the suburbs they were resisting a Japanese attack. For the first time in her life she had heard the crash of artillery, felt the earth shake and the acrid smoke in her lungs – and seen men carried from the line on stretchers, broken and bleeding.

And now Richard was upstairs, meeting secretly with several Chinese agents, Ozaki the Japanese and two Europeans she had never seen before. It was her duty to keep watch and she was nervous; in a city on the verge of war everyone was jumpy and there were too many different enemies to look out for – the municipal police, Chiang's terrifying thugs, Nationalist soldiers. Europeans could now be in as much danger as Chinese. Only a few months ago another Comintern agent, Hilaire Noulens, and his wife had been arrested and sentenced to death. In the end the Centre had provided twenty thousand dollars to bribe the Chinese judge and their sentences had been commuted to life imprisonment, with an understanding that they would soon be released and deported to Moscow. But they had been lucky. It would not be so easy for anyone caught now, with the Japanese outside the city.

She studied the sleeping baby for some time, leaning forward to touch the perfection of his tiny hand as it grasped the edge of his shawl. Sonia was no longer afraid to die if necessary, but Ruth still had powerful reasons for living. Rocking the cradle again, she opened the door for a short patrol of the garden.

It was cold outside and she threw a coat around her shoulders for warmth. The tree-lined street was silent as usual, except for a group of men a hundred yards away. There were about eight of them, brandishing rifles with bayonets, shouting and reeling as if drunk. Two were hammering on the door of a European house, which finally fell inwards. They vanished inside and Ruth heard crashes of wood and glass breaking.

She froze with fear. Blueshirts rarely ventured into the international quarter. This must be a group who had got drunk and turned to looting; but they would not be too drunk to arrest a group of Europeans and Chinese Communists in a conspiratorial meeting – or, more likely, to shoot them on the spot. There was no time to think before they were pouring in through the gate from the road. She stood her ground imperiously and addressed them in her sparse Chinese. 'You have no right to enter here. Show me your authority; what do you want?'

The leader was burly, cradling a carbine in heavily muscled arms. His blue shirt was open to the waist and he wore a Nationalist flag knotted round his head. He thrust his face close to hers and she recoiled from the vicious eyes and breath that stank of beer and rotting teeth. 'Stand aside,' he hissed, waving the carbine menacingly.

'No! You have no right to be here – this house is owned by a German diplomat.' It wasn't true but it was worth a try. He did not move and she screamed at him. 'You heard what I said! Get out of here!' His arm swung from the shoulder and she felt a stinging slap on her cheek. Biting back tears, she reeled and turned to face him again. 'How dare you – get out before I call the police!' He responded by kicking her to the ground and she shielded her head in her arms as their boots clattered past, one catching her a sickening blow on the shoulder. Then there was the crack of a shot and dead silence.

Kneeling up, she saw Richard on the verandah holding a pistol. She smelt the cordite as he fired again. Now he was aiming directly at the leader, but no one fired back. He sprang down the steps, waving the gun and roaring in the local dialect. To her astonishment the blueshirts suddenly turned, filed out of the gate and started to run away. Richard aimed two shots into the dust of the road to speed them on.

She fell into his arms and kissed him, feeling the warm metal of the pistol in his hand against her back. 'Thank God you came.'

'Are you hurt?'

'No – just a few bruises.'

'Sure?'

'Quite sure.'

He smiled. 'I'm proud of you, Ruth. You were incredibly brave.'

'But why didn't they shoot you?'

'Too drunk – or they had no bullets. The blueshirts have been short of ammunition for weeks and I took a gamble on their guns being just for show. After all they were looting, probably deserters.'

'But you could have been killed.'

'We could *both* have been killed,' he said solemnly. 'And I must get rid of the others. Those thugs won't come back, but the police might turn up to investigate.'

Ten minutes later she sighed in relief as she heard them leave at intervals by the back door. She mounted the stairs to join Sorge, who was now alone, and they sat on cushions by the window, looking towards the river where the air raid had ended with the usual pyre of billowing black smoke.

'Is there anyone outside?'

She shook her head. 'No police and no one suspicious. I think we are quite safe.'

25

They sipped bowls of green tea and the tension of the last half hour started to evaporate. 'If you're sure you are not hurt, Ruth, can you bear to consider Mr Carteret for a few minutes?'

'Of course.'

'Tell me about him, then. Perhaps the time has come for a report to Moscow? How old is he?'

'About twenty-six.'

'Unmarried?'

'He says he is single – he shares an apartment with another man.'

'Homosexual?'

She laughed. 'Oh no – I'm certain he's not.'

'How do you know?'

'Richard! We've danced together at parties and I can tell from the way he holds me – and from the way he looks at me when we play tennis. He is a year older than me and I think he quite fancies me. A woman can sense such things.'

'Have you slept with him?'

'Certainly not.'

Sorge stroked her cheek gently. 'I just wondered, you look so fetching in that white tennis dress.'

She giggled. 'Carteret is perfectly normal, but I have no wish to make love with him. For one thing he drinks too much and always smells of cigarettes and alcohol.'

'But can you confirm that he's no longer a journalist? That he works now for British American Tobacco?'

'That's right.'

'Have you talked about Oxford with him?'

'Yes. He seems rather ambivalent about it – but he is very keen on golf and played for the university.'

Sorge shook his head. 'No, he didn't; I have a report from comrades in London. I suspect he is just boasting to impress you. He also stayed at Oxford less than two years and left with no degree. That would suggest he is lazy or stupid – yet he has made the effort to come to China and puts great energy into making a living here. Can you explain that?'

'He says he came to China, the other side of the world, to escape from his awful family and from the Church.'

'The Church?'

'His father is an Anglican bishop, of somewhere called Taunton.'

'Amazing, but it still makes too little sense – what are his political views?'

'He is not a socialist.'

'Is he *anything*?'

Sonia considered the question, staring out of the window while Sorge stroked her thigh through the thin cotton of her dress. She turned to him with amused eyes. 'In England he would probably be a conservative.'

'How unoriginal . . . but has he flaws? Is he vulnerable?'

'Perhaps, but I cannot see that he would be of interest to the Fourth Bureau.'

'You cannot know what purposes the Centre may have, Ruth.' Suddenly he looked at her sternly. 'Tomorrow you will write – and code – a full report.'

Primly she sat bolt upright. 'Of course, Dr Sorge.' She eyed him provocatively and her throaty laughter gave way to a slow smile as he took her in his arms and carried her to the couch.

Sorge lay half asleep and she caressed his hard chest and flanks, averting her eyes from the scars on his legs. They had both been broken by shrapnel when he was twenty-one, serving in the German army in the First World War. They had given him the Iron Cross for it, but sometimes her poor Richard – so masculine, so confident, so commanding – limped like an old man or flinched with pain like a little boy. Tenderly she kissed his closed eyes.

The bathroom had a long mirror, which reflected her own unscarred body, firm and slender – downright skinny to many of Rolf's German friends who liked their women matronly and bovine. Her arms and legs showed the slight swell of powerful muscles and she was tanned brown all over, except for a strip across her buttocks and loins, so white that it was almost obscene. She smiled wryly. Her face was too round and she would have liked, so much, to be beautiful. But Richard said that she had now become a captain in the Red Army – and it was a practical kind of body, suitable for a soldier. It would serve.

6

Caux-sur-Montreux – 1940

Sonia and Len were married on 23 February, 1940, the twenty-second birthday of the Red Army. It was a simple occasion, as befitted a paper marriage ordered by the Centre. They bought a cheap ring at a one-price emporium in Vevey on the way to the registrar, then took a taxi back to Sonia's chalet in Caux.

Len opened a bottle of champagne, while Olga Muth – Sonia's childhood nurse and now brought from Berlin as her housekeeper – prepared lunch with glowering disapproval. The children fled from the atmosphere and played in Micha's bedroom. When Olga finally banged two Spanish omelettes on the dining table Len looked uncomfortable, but Sonia collapsed with laughter. 'Poor Ollo,' she chuckled when they were alone. 'She liked Rolf and thinks I'm a disgraceful scarlet woman.'

'Didn't you tell her you were marrying me just because I'm British? To get a British passport?'

'Yes, but I don't think she believed me.' Sonia took his arm and they walked out to the balcony, champagne glasses in hand. The mountain air was cold, their breath forming small clouds of mist as she smiled up at him. 'I'm not sure I believe it any more myself.'

The timbers of the balcony creaked as they moved and below their feet the hillside fell away to the clustered chalets of Montreux, then on down to the icy blue of the lake. Sonia had rented *La Taupinière* because it was so high up and gave her clear radio transmission over the necessary one and a half thousand miles; she had recruited Len Beurton, along with Alexander Foote, from British Communists who had fought in the Spanish civil war. Both Len and the chalet

28

were part of her espionage equipment but today would be a holiday; for once she could relax and enjoy them a little.

Len put his arm round her. He was a handsome enough young man, clean-cut, very English and seven years younger. At first Sonia, now thirty-three, had felt almost maternal towards him. It was all so different from China, when she had been young, girlish, bowled over by Sorge's dash and masculinity, his total command and confidence. Ten years had passed since then and she had served in Poland, Nazi Germany and Switzerland. There had been other lovers and another child, but she could never recapture the heart-tearing happiness she had known in Shanghai. She sighed and, even today, sensed the smarting well of tears always hidden below the surface.

Len did not notice the pretty, vivacious face stiffen nor see the sudden opaqueness in her eyes. He drained his glass and made to kiss her. Ever since their first contact in Geneva he had found her attractive: a cheerful extrovert with a good figure and even better legs, black hair cut with misleading demureness. She might be a lieutenant-colonel and his senior officer in the Red Army, but today she was also his wife. She flinched slightly as their lips met and he drew back. 'Is something the matter?'

'No, Len, nothing. I don't get married every day and it has made me pensive, that's all.' She gave a bleak little smile and sighed. Soon, too soon, she would be on the move again, for the biggest task yet. She did not know the details, but it involved going to Britain, at war with Germany since last September. Hence the divorce from Rolf, the tight-lipped hostility of Ollo, and a *marriage blanche* to this personable young Englishman who did not yet know her real name, let alone whether she was any good in bed. Suddenly she felt his arm round her shoulders and realized that he was speaking. 'Sorry – what did you say, Len?'

'I said tomorrow you must go to the British Consulate to apply for a passport, Mrs Beurton.'

And then, she thought grimly, I must set off with the children on that frightful train journey to Spain, and then to Lisbon to look for a ship, leaving you to carry on here. With a surge of determination she pushed the past and future away and smiled up at him, brown eyes flashing provocatively. 'But fortunately tomorrow is a long way off.'

The sea passage from Lisbon took longer than she expected, for they first set out in a convoy of twelve freighters steaming towards Gibraltar. The ship had dim blue lights in the cabins and the covers of all the portholes were bolted shut because of the blackout and the threat from German submarines. Every passenger was issued with a cork lifebelt and ordered to carry it at all times.

The final run across the Bay of Biscay was rough and the physical misery blocked out all other preoccupations. The two children shared a tiny, hot cabin with Sonia, alternately being seasick and huddling to her for comfort. For the last few hours the wind dropped and they slept, both under a blanket in one bunk. Sonia went on deck alone as the ship steamed into Liverpool. It was 1941, a bitterly cold January dawn, and the city looked unwelcoming in the grey half-light. When the ship had docked a party of officials came on board; they were equally unwelcoming as the two dozen passengers lined up in the saloon. Two men in civilian clothes sat at a deal table, two soldiers with fixed bayonets standing behind them.

A third soldier, a corporal, summoned each passenger to stand in front of the table. Most were dealt with rapidly, but Sonia felt an eel of fear wriggling in her stomach when her turn came. Micha stood by her confidently, but Nina clung to her skirt and started to cry. 'Shut that child up,' snapped one of the men at the table; he had a florid face, handlebar moustache and watery eyes.

Sonia comforted her daughter. 'I'm sorry, but she is only five.' Awkwardly she fished inside her coat for her passport and handed it over, clutching Nina with the other arm.

'Just keep her quiet. We've no time to waste – there's a war on and we've four more ships to check.' He studied her new passport. 'I see you were born in Berlin, Mrs Beurton.' His eyes searched her face suspiciously. 'You are an enemy alien.'

'No – I am a British citizen. My husband is British.'

'And where is this husband?'

'He is still in Switzerland and will follow later.'

'In *Switzerland*? Follow *later* will he? I don't quite understand – why didn't he come with you?'

'He has a job and must finish his contract. Then he plans to come home and join the army.'

'Join the army will he?' The man spoke with a disbelieving sneer. 'So why have you come first? Why didn't you stay with him until he was ready to travel?'

He knows nothing, she told herself, he is just trying to rattle me in case I have something to hide. 'I have come to find us somewhere to live,' she answered firmly. 'And to see my parents, who are Jewish refugees from Germany.'

'Really – and just who *are* these parents? What is their address?'

'Dr and Mrs René Kuczynski. They live at 25a Upper Park Road, London NW3.'

'I see.' He wrote slowly in a khaki notebook. 'And how do you plan to earn your living with no husband to support you?'

'I have enough money to manage until he joins me.'

'Let me see.' Without asking permission he opened her handbag, took out the bundle of notes and counted them. 'One hundred pounds will not last very long.'

'My parents will take care of us.'

'Hmn.' He seemed about to ask another question when Sonia put Nina down; she immediately buried her face in her mother's side and started to howl loudly. The immigration officer looked pained and Sonia smiled at him. 'I'm sorry. She's frightened and she was very sick on the crossing.'

'Oh God, really? Well – you'd better go ashore, hadn't you?' Hurriedly he stamped the passport and handed her a stencilled note. 'This will explain wartime travel regulations to you. The penalties for infringement are severe. I take it you are going to London?' She nodded and he gave a ghastly smile. 'When you arrive report to the police for gasmasks. In the meantime have a pleasant journey.'

Ten minutes later she was on the quay. There was no taxi and she set out wearily towards the station, past the long line of warehouses guarded by soldiers with tommy-guns. Sonia carried the two suitcases, Nina clinging to her

31

sleeve and Micha walking independently with his own small case.

They could not get a train to Oxford until next day and their compartment was crowded with soldiers, kitbags piled in the corridor. Nina won the heart of one of them, who made a gun like his with her plasticine. When he took off his battledress top, the children gaped in wonder at his tattoos. Nina wanted to be tattooed herself, so he spat on her small plump arm and drew with an indelible pencil, then offered Sonia his copy of the *Daily Express* and played cards with the boy.

The newspaper was of coarse, wartime paper and only four pages long. Sonia glanced at the headlines and felt her face drain of colour: *GERMAN PARACHUTE SPY EXECUTED*. The print blurred as she read on. *A German Secret Service agent was executed at Pentonville Prison yesterday morning* . . . It was a brief account of an incompetent Sudeten German dropped into Hertfordshire by parachute and captured after a couple of days – a silly, sad little story, but all the same now he was in a lime-pit with a paper shroud and a broken neck.

When her eyes re-focused she could not stop reading it again and again. They hanged traitors too . . . and she was now a British subject. That was how she had got into the country. Being a woman would not save her, for a traitor was worse than a spy. If they caught her, they would hang her. Of course she had always known that, the Centre had told her months ago, but suddenly it seemed terrifyingly real – and what would happen then to these two trusting children, Nina asleep beside her and Micha playing cards with the Tommy like two old men in a Berlin café? She tried to suppress the gnawing pincers of fear and stared pensively at the green fields outside the train window.

7

Oxford – 1941

For the first few weeks Sonia lodged with the family of the Reverend Charles Cox, rector of Glympton, a village near Oxford, then she found a furnished bungalow to rent in Kidlington three miles outside the city. She had received details of her first contact before leaving Switzerland and kept the assignation as directed, on a street in London near Hyde Park. No one turned up. Dutifully she went to the same place a week later, but again no one arrived.

Three months passed in this way, until she was desperate for both instructions and money, fearing that the Centre had abandoned her. In May she took the train to Paddington feeling low and depressed and again walked the short distance to the *Treffpunkt*. This time a man spoke to her on the pavement with the pre-arranged code-words and she walked two streets further to meet another man who introduced himself as Sergei. They went to a Lyons tea shop and he handed her an envelope containing three hundred pounds.

'I'm sorry for the delay,' he said in English. 'I had a car accident. Let us have some tea and then we will go for a walk in Hyde Park – there is much to discuss and I have important work for you. Also this.' He handed her a package about a foot long and six inches square. It was heavy and she guessed that the brown paper concealed a radio transceiver. 'A new model,' he smiled. 'Small but very powerful. The best there is.'

It was not until August that Sonia's train journeys changed direction. Early one Sunday she left the children with her mother, who had stayed the night at the bungalow, and cycled into Oxford. Not far from the station an angry crowd was shouting outside a house with broken windows. Two policemen were shepherding out a man, a woman and two small boys, about five or six years old. There was a chorus of booing and several bricks were thrown. One of the boys fell, screaming, bleeding from the scalp.

'Stop that!' roared one of the police, drawing his truncheon. 'They've done you no harm.'

'Bloody Boche, aren't they?' The atmosphere of fear and hate was electric.

'What's going on?' Sonia asked a woman at the back of the crowd as the animal baying increased.

'There was a nasty air raid on Cowley last night. Lot of people killed.'

'But surely those people are refugees from Hitler?'

The woman shrugged. 'Still Boche, ain't they? So far as I'm concerned the only good German's a dead 'un.'

The burly policeman had stopped shouting and picked the boy up in his arms. The child's face was white and his tiny limbs hung down motionlessly. The German woman was sobbing in her husband's arms. There was a lull in the catcalls and the other constable raised his arm. 'Let us through peaceably,' his strained voice seemed to echo in the silence. 'The little boy has died.'

In Banbury, Sonia left the station and walked several miles along country lanes into the Chilterns, occasionally glancing at a sketch-map that she would destroy later. It was hot and she was sweating by the time she reached the *Treffpunkt* – but he was waiting there, on the corner of two country roads, just as Sergei had said.

He was about thirty, with a nondescript tweed jacket and a smooth, nondescript face. She saw a domed forehead, receding hair and pale blue eyes behind rimless spectacles. She smiled at him and spoke in German: 'The substitution of the proletarian for the bourgeois state is impossible.'

'Without a violent revolution.' He did not smile and looked distinctly nervous.

'That is a quotation from Engels.'

'No – it is a quotation from Lenin.'

'So it is. Who sent you?'

'Sergei, you must know that. I assume it is a code-name – I don't know what he is really called.'

She raised her eyebrows. 'You should not depart from the agreed code-words, but welcome!' She seized his hands and clasped them warmly. *'Wie geht's Ihnen, Genosse Klaus?'*

'Gut, danke – und Ihnen?' They strolled along the lane until they came to a stile. She vaulted over it lightly and he followed; on the other side was a footpath running down a wooded valley by a stream.

'How long have you been in England?'

'Since 1933. The Gestapo were after me and I was in hiding in Germany for five months, but managed to escape that September. I was looked after by a family in Bristol.'

'And you have worked in theoretical physics in universities ever since?'

'Yes. Before the Nazis came I studied physics at Kiel. In Britain I worked at Bristol and Edinburgh, until they interned me in Canada last summer. I was released and shipped back in January.'

'And then they invited you to join the team at Birmingham University?'

'That's right. I came down from Birmingham by train today.'

So far Sonia had only asked questions to which she already knew the answer. There was no reason to believe that the man was not Klaus Fuchs, but it did no harm to check. They sat down beside the stream. 'I've brought some cheese sandwiches,' she said. 'Would you like one?'

He nodded hungrily. 'Thank you. I missed my breakfast.'

'Tell me about this Birmingham project.'

'I gave Sergei the details, you know – for you I have brought copies of papers to go back to the Centre.'

'Tell me anyway.'

He shrugged. 'There is so much to say . . . it is secret and code-named Tube Metals, it is run by the government . . . it will take a long time.'

'But what is the objective?'

'It is to apply the principles of nuclear fission to a weapon.'

'I don't understand.'

'Do you know about atomic theory?'

'A little.' Sonia munched a cheese sandwich, eyeing a sheep on the other bank lowering its head to drink from the stream. The grass was dappled with patches of sun and shade.

'The same theory will be applied to produce an explosive – a bomb. A bomb based on uranium rather than TNT. They call it an atomic bomb.'

Sonia yawned; she was starting to feel drowsy in the heat. 'Is it important? How much damage could such a bomb inflict?'

'A single bomb could destroy a large area – probably a whole city – by blast and fire.'

'A whole *city*?' Her eyes widened. 'Are you serious? One bomb could destroy a city? Then ten or twenty could blitz a whole country?'

'That's right.'

'My God. Let me see these papers.' Fuchs handed her an envelope from his inside pocket and she scanned its contents. The sheets of lined foolscap, each headed by a roughly printed royal arms in light blue, were covered in mathematical formulae. There were also pages of notes in a neat, crabbed hand. 'You copied these out yourself?'

'I *calculated* most of it myself, but the notes are mine too.'

She laughed, now wide awake again. 'Of course. You know, Klaus, I think we should walk a little further; I think perhaps we have some plans to make.'

8

Oxford – 1942

Their office was a Nissen hut in the grounds of Blenheim Palace. Inside, the narrow building was divided up by wood and plasterboard partitions standing on a concrete floor. They were part of F Division; at one end of the hut was the cubby-hole occupied by Jack Carteret as head of section F1(a), at the other sat Richard Fell, head of F1(b). Carteret dealt with subversion by communists and Fell with subversion by fascists. A typist and six clerks worked in the large room in the middle of the hut.

Despite wartime petrol rationing, both men were allowed to run cars and used them daily to travel from their rented houses in Oxford. Both of them were somewhat withdrawn, and it was rumoured that there was a friendly rivalry between them, but occasionally they would go to the Marlborough Arms in the village for a pint together early in the evening: Fell tall and upright, Carteret hunched and round-shouldered.

On one such evening they were accompanied by two others from the office and the session broke up at about eight o'clock. Three cars left the pub in Woodstock, one taking a circuitous route back into the suburbs of Oxford. The driver was alone. He steered the black Austin Ten along twisting country lanes until he came to the ruins of a barn butting on to the roadway; its roof had gone and the stonework was cracked. He left the car and fumbled in a crack near the ground. It was autumn and almost dusk, so there was little danger of being seen, but as a precaution he did not open the envelope until he had driven three miles further on. The message was short: details of a new drop where he was to leave the classified documents he copied each night,

37

and instructions for a meeting with a woman agent in a few days' time.

Sonia collected Fuchs' material at regular intervals, usually in the lanes around Banbury: once a month or more frequently if Tube Metals was moving fast. It was too bulky and its content too technical for transmission by radio, so she carried it into London by train to go in the diplomatic bag, meeting Sergei in the open spaces accessible from Paddington. Sometimes it was Hyde Park, sometimes Wormwood Scrubs or a convenient cemetery, but never the same place twice in a row.

She had moved into Oxford, renting a converted coach-house called Avenue Cottage in George Street, Summertown. Len had returned to England and joined the army. She was alone with the children unpacking when the police came, hammering loudly on the front door.

It was nine o'clock on a Saturday morning and two men in blue tunics and police helmets stood on the step. She smiled at them, but they stared at her grimly and she began to feel sick inside. One had a sergeant's chevrons on his sleeve. 'May we come in?' He stepped over the threshold without waiting for an answer.

'What can I do for you?' She tried to look as housewifely as possible, folding her trembling hands together under her apron.

'I believe you have just moved in?'

'That's right. We used to live outside Oxford.'

'And you are of German nationality.'

'Not at all. I am German by birth, but married to an Englishman who is in the army, so I am a British subject.'

'Do you have an identity card?'

'Certainly – you can see my marriage certificate and passport as well, if you like.'

'Produce them.' He was making no effort to be friendly and she suddenly remembered with horror that her short-wave radio set was in full view on the bureau upstairs in her bedroom. Fortunately the aerial was not strung outside.

'Please wait in the kitchen and I'll get them.' She hurried upstairs and closed the bedroom door firmly behind her, cursing that it had no lock. It took a minute or two to ease up the floorboard, from which she had removed the nails yesterday, and slide the transmitter underneath to rest on the pieces of wood she had jammed between the joists. She had intended to nail the board down properly if there was danger of a search, but today she could only cover it with a rug and hope for the best.

She seized the papers from her desk and returned to the kitchen. The policemen examined each document carefully, especially the Swiss marriage certificate – it was in French and plainly they could not read it – and her passport. The sergeant pulled a notebook from his breast pocket and wrote in it. 'What is your husband's unit in the army?'

'The first armoured battalion of the Coldstream Guards.'

'Where is he stationed?'

'I am not sure. He is training in a secret location and I have not seen him for a month. I have to write to him at a forces' box number.'

'Write it down for me, with his full name, rank and number.'

When she had done so, the sergeant replaced his helmet. Sonia almost fainted with relief as he turned to go.

'Thank you, madam. Just routine, you know – as an alien you should have reported your change of address to the police station.' Sonia stopped trembling and went back to the two children, who had ignored the visitors and continued to play in the living room. It had been a painful lesson in security; she would never be so lax with her radio set again. That night she reported the visit in her transmission to Moscow and three days later she received a reply. When decoded it read: *Against the danger of arrest train and brief substitute operator. Mechanic code-name Steve from Cowley armoured car factory appears suitable. Leave spare radio for him in secure emergency drop and report arrangements to Centre.*

She was waiting for the man from MI5 in a gateway on the Woodstock Road. He drove the Austin Ten into the shelter of the wood she had chosen, its tyres crunching on dead leaves and fir cones, backing it into some bushes to conceal the distinctive divided rear window, then walked slowly back towards her. She held out her hand and he grasped it eagerly. 'I am Alec.' He looked grey and worried – or perhaps just tired.

'I am Sonia.' She put her arm through his, so that to any passing observer they would look like lovers, and led him down a woodland path. After a few questions about his work, which she knew in some depth already, she turned to him abruptly. 'Tell me, Alec – would your Division F know of any suspicion attaching to a man or woman working for the government? Say a scientist?'

'Not necessarily. There are other divisions – B for counter-espionage and C for security – which might well handle that. F is more concerned with political parties and agitators.'

'But if there was one particular scientist who had become a valuable asset for us – working, say, on a secret weapons project – could you arrange to be informed if *he* came under suspicion?'

'It would be difficult, but if I had his name and all the details . . . then, yes, I might be able to devise a way.'

She smiled. 'Good.' She would not mention Fuchs' name at this meeting; she would need the Centre's clearance for that. 'It may be very important to protect one of our sources in the next year or so, so tell me – how might that be done?' They had reached the edge of the wood and set out across an open field in the grey light of dusk.

She had sat up all night, waiting for the dawn, but it was still dark outside when the silence was broken by jangling keys. The cell door clanged open and a small man in a blue suit bustled in, flanked by two male warders.

She stood up shakily, her throat suddenly dry with terror. She had rejected the priest's offer to stay with her in the small hours, but now she saw him in the doorway and wanted to run to him like a frightened child. Instead she swayed weakly, her limbs paralysed with fear, and made no resistance as they strapped her wrists tightly behind her back. Like an automaton she lurched through the door, half supported by the two warders gripping her arms. The execution chamber was painted a muddy green and lit by naked bulbs which dazzled her eyes. She saw a blur of black figures and strained white faces.

She could not move, overwhelmed by confusion and disbelief, but they pushed her forward roughly. When she saw the noose dangling level with her eyes she wanted to cry out, but could not. Mesmerized by the menacing circle of hemp covered in wash-leather, she realized that she was standing on the trap and hands were strapping her legs. Suddenly a white bag was placed over her head, shutting out the light, and she felt the rope chafing on her neck.

She woke with a scream, bathed in sweat, and it was some minutes before she realized that she was still in Avenue Cottage with the children asleep in the other room. She pulled on her dressing gown and went down to the kitchen where she drank a glass of cold water. Turning off the light because of the blackout she opened the door and looked out into the street. The white houses lay sleeping in the moonlight, peacefully as ever, and an ARP warden in a tin hat was patrolling the pavement under the trees.

9

Oxford – 1945

8 May, 1945 – VE Day. The war in Europe was over and a
street party was hurriedly organized in George Street.
Trestle tables had been arranged outside a row of lock-up
garages, decorated with small Union Jacks and roses from
the gardens. Despite food rationing and only one egg a week
per person, the tables were covered with cakes and large
pots of tea. The two boys and Nina played games with the
English children and Sonia chatted with strangers. Len was
still in Germany with the army.

Shortly afterwards the owner of Avenue Cottage returned
from the war and Sonia had to move; she found a cottage
to rent in the village of Great Rollright, near Chipping
Norton in the Cotswolds. The situation was ideal: only
twenty miles north of Oxford and not too far from the
nuclear research centre at Harwell, but off the main roads
and as remote as if it were in Cumberland or Cornwall. The
cottage had once been a farmhouse and its L-shape enclosed
a small yard hidden from the road. The walls were of stone
and the sagging roof of slate. It was surrounded by high
conifers and called The Firs.

In August came the news that an atomic bomb had been
dropped on Hiroshima, then a few days later a second on
Nagasaki. Sonia knew that this must be the result of the
work Klaus Fuchs had been engaged on, although she had
not seen him for over two years. He had been sent to
continue his research in America and her last duty had been
to give him instructions on making contact with a new
controller, on a street corner in New York.

It was more than a week after the surrender of Japan that
she went shopping in Oxford. There were a couple of hours

42

to kill before she caught the local train back to the halt near Great Rollright, so she slipped into a cinema: she hadn't seen a film for years.

The newsreel took her by surprise. After film of the Japanese surrender to General MacArthur on a warship in Tokyo Bay, there was a sudden switch to the brilliant flash and white cloud rising over Nagasaki: filmed from the observer aircraft. Then there were disjointed clips taken by rescue teams hours after the bombing. It was appalling. Men and women naked, covered in burns; some with slices of blackened skin hanging from bodies flayed raw by the heat, others clutching children, hopelessly trying to deaden their agony by crowding into the water of a river. Inhuman faces that were staring masks of terror . . . human heat shadows burnt on concrete walls . . . the ruins of the cathedral that had been almost under the centre of the explosion. More American Army film showed the total devastation: blast and firestorm had razed a flat plain where there had been a city, mile after mile of rubble, smoking and broken up by the twisted steel skeletons of buildings. A queue of dying Chinese prisoners – the camera moved quickly away from a group of Australians – sores open to the sun, waited outside a dressing station in a ruined school. So that was what it had all been about. She left before the main film started, feeling slightly sick.

Alec had returned to an office in London, but some of his staff were still in Nissen huts in the grounds of Blenheim and he visited them each week, leaving papers for Sonia in one of the dead letter drops. She had strung a looping wire aerial in the branches of the trees around the cottage and kept her radio hidden in a cavity under the steps down to the cellar. Twice a week she transmitted from there, usually in the early hours of the morning by the light of the bulb she had hung from the worm-eaten beams.

Sonia received her instructions by radio or through a *dubok* on the Oxford-Banbury road. When she cycled from Great Rollright, it was after a railway bridge and a crossroads, under an exposed root of the fourth tree on the left. Late in the summer she received an order to meet Sergei in

43

London – 'Sergei's' identity had changed during the war, but the code-name had not – and found that she was to meet Alec face to face again, for only the second time in four years. 'You are to meet him secretly,' Sergei had said, as they strode across the barren common at Wormwood Scrubs. 'Report on his mental attitudes. Is he still committed, confident, secure?'

It took several weeks to arrange, but they met early one evening in a wood a few miles from Blenheim. Sonia was shocked by Alec's appearance. He looked harassed and nervous, older than a man in his early forties, and as if he drank habitually and too much. She found a clearing where they could sit and eyed him questioningly. 'You look very tired, Alec.'

He sat down beside her, awkward in his stiff grey suit. 'We are still working desperately hard even though the war is over – too much information, too little time to analyse it.'

'But you look strained, as well.'

He flushed, then turned to face her. '"Strained"? My God, yes I feel "strained".' The words came tumbling out. 'I've been feeding you with sensitive material for *four years* now and the risk is getting to me. When I'm rational about it, I think I'm probably safe enough, but there is no one I can ever *talk* to. I cannot tell my wife – not that she would care anyway – nor my friends. No one. I feel so alone I sometimes feel I'm going mad. I want to scream in the street, "I'm a traitor, *I'm a bloody commie traitor* . . ." do you understand?'

He gave a sheepish smile and she saw that his hands were shaking. She realized why the Centre had required a meeting and took his hands firmly in hers, leaning forward to kiss him lightly on the forehead. 'You're a brave man, Alec, and we need you badly. It must be lonely, terrifying – will I do as a friend to tell about it?'

He started to pour out his hopes and fears and she listened solicitously, wishing that she felt less ambivalent towards this unhappy Englishman. Of course he had taken grave risks, of course he was a comrade; but she felt irritated by his upper-class accent and his gentleman's clothes. It was all too remote from China, from what she had seen in Russia.

She resented listening to the fears of a man who had so much less courage than her beloved Sorge, but she must find a way to give him strength and reassurance. Whatever happened she must not lose him; the success of the Centre's most vital operation in Britain depended on it.

Two weeks later he looked better. He was less nervous and did not smell of alcohol. He still spoke of his fear of discovery, but more rationally and with less self-pity. She suppressed her ambivalence as they walked through fields and towards the deserted barn she had earmarked earlier in the week. She grasped his hand and he kept hold of her, as if it gave him comfort. It was dusk when they reached the little stone building, where she had left a rug the previous day.

She had not quite decided what was to happen then, but when he turned to her in the half-light she knew.

'Thank you,' he said, holding her close to him. 'I think I shall be all right now.'

He said nothing when she laid the rug on the straw in a corner of the barn, smoothing out its wrinkles with one hand while she held his with the other. A gentle pull and he lay beside her, smiling at her body as she knelt up to open her blouse and slip her knickers off. 'You are a brave man, Alec,' she whispered, now astride and leaning down to kiss him. In her mind she sensed that he had never discarded his trousers for a woman outside the security of a bedroom before, and almost laughed, but continued to caress his face and loins until suddenly he responded and clung to her.

Deliberately she pushed away the black thoughts that he did not know her name, nor where she lived, nor whether she had a husband, that she mistrusted and despised him, that at first something about him had made her body go frigid. Her knees gripped his sides and she made love to him with all the femininity and vigour she could summon, twisting and plunging her hips as she whispered endearments and his hands moved from her shoulders, stroking her back, to grasp her buttocks fiercely and press her down to him.

*

45

It was nine months later and a hot summer when the blow fell. A meeting with Sergei was rare, so she took the train to Paddington with a light heart. Leaving the terminus with its great glass roof, she caught the District Line to West Brompton and made for the *Treffpunkt* in the overgrown cemetery. Sergei was waiting for her. She did not know that in a matter of seconds he was to shatter her world for ever.

PART THREE

The Recent Future

10

Brussels

Sarah Cable edged the hired Renault 5 from the traffic snarl-up in Rue de la Loi and turned into a side street. Following Nairn's laconic directions, she picked up speed between the high buildings, tyres drumming on the cobbles, twisting and turning until she felt completely lost. His knowledge of the back streets of every European capital never ceased to amaze her.

'Turn left at the top,' he said, glancing at her sideways as they crossed the Square de Meeus. It was two years since Sarah had joined the service, after her first encounter with Nairn in a hospital in Austria.* With her slight build and long fair hair she still looked young, but he noted the firmer jawline with approval. He had also come to respect the shrewd intelligence that shone through those grey eyes, sometimes full of laughter, now grave as she concentrated. Six months ago she had joined the small staff that handled special projects for him, as a finishing school before her first posting abroad.

'Turn right, Sarah,' he closed his eyes as they narrowly missed a yellow tram, 'and park in this little square.'

'Where are we? I've been lost ever since we turned off the motorway from the airport.'

'The Place de Londres. We're meeting him in that joint in the corner, the one with the sign saying Musée de la Bière.'

'The *beer* museum? I don't believe it!'

Nairn laughed. 'It's just a bar, but the owner has a sense of humour. Go in and find a table; you'll recognize our

* See *Seven Steps to Treason* by Michael Hartland

49

friend from the FBI photograph when he arrives. I'll wait in the car to make sure he isn't followed. It's primitive as security, but it will have to do.'

Sarah nodded. 'Okay. What do I do when he turns up?'

'You've got the little transmitter in your handbag?'

'Of course.'

'I'll listen in while you start to talk to him. When you're sure he's serious – or as sure as you can be in ten minutes – take him across the road to the block of flats with the striped awning over the front door.' He gave her a key. 'Our people rent apartment 207. Wait for me there. The key opens the street door as well.'

'Suppose we're stopped by the concierge?'

'You won't be. She's usually legless on gin by this time of day, but if she happens to be awake it's a nice anonymous place and she'll just think you're on the game.'

'Thanks a lot!' Sarah swung her legs out on to the pavement and unfolded, like a young colt, to her full height of five feet ten inches. Eyes turned with approval as she entered the café.

The Musée de la Bière had panelled walls stained dark brown by years of tobacco smoke, broken up by gilt-framed mirrors. Brass lamps hung from the ceiling and the furniture, though not actually bolted to the floor, was otherwise such as one might find in a maximum security prison. The place was crowded and, through the blue haze of tobacco, Sarah saw that the East German was already there, sitting alone on a sagging leather bench in the corner.

'May I join you?' She spoke in German; she had become fluent in the language while living in Vienna, but had worked since joining the service to achieve a mastery and an accent that would let her pass for a native. 'You must be Dr Werner? My name is Ingrid.'

His face had a pink, well-scrubbed texture and he eyed her furtively. He was about forty, but his receding hair was already grey. 'You are from London? You sound like a Berliner.'

'Thank you but don't worry, I *am* from London. Would you like another beer?'

'If we can get served.' He gave a thin-lipped smile and

gestured towards the red-shirted Congolese barmaid, floating through the bar with languid grace, ignoring the customers calling for service, occasionally taking away the overflowing ashtrays and forgetting to return them. But without being bidden a man behind the bar pulled two beers and brought them over; he was unshaven and wore a blue pullover full of holes, eyeing Sarah with undisguised lust.

She smiled at the German again. 'What a jolly place, it was clever of you to choose it. May I call you Peter?'

'Please do.'

'I always think Belgians have a look of quiet desperation, don't you? It must be the result of everything being in two languages and everyone smelling of chips.'

He sipped his beer. 'Please – there is no time for polite conversation, nor for any more delays. What the hell is going on?'

'What do you mean?'

'For God's sake!' His voice rose dangerously high but was lost in the hubbub of the bar. 'I go to the FBI in San Francisco and offer to defect, but what happens? They do nothing and tell me you will make contact in Brussels. So I hang about here three days at Geli's apartment and what happens? Nothing.'

'I'm here now.'

'But I am in danger, *grave* danger, and a whole week has been wasted! Unless we can arrange something tonight I am supposed to fly back to Berlin tomorrow. Are your people going to help us or not? I *must* know.'

At about the same time, a green Vauxhall drew up outside a modern bungalow in a village near Milton Keynes in Buckinghamshire. It stood in a new cul-de-sac of red-tiled houses and bungalows, incongruously sandwiched between the village inn and the tower of the fourteenth-century church. A middle-aged man wearing a cavalry tie and three-piece suit got out and walked up the garden path in the dusk. He rang the bell and the door was opened by a tall man who eyed him unwelcomingly.

'Good evening, Richard,' smiled the visitor. 'Another month has passed. May I come in?'

51

'If you must. I've nothing to say to you.'

'Yes, I must. You've nothing new to tell me? How disappointing – but never mind, I always enjoy our little chats.'

'What the hell do you want with me after twenty years? Haven't you done enough damage already?'

'They just want to keep in touch, old chap. As I've said before, I'd prefer you to regard me as a friend of the family.'

Sarah drew the curtains at the window which looked down on the dark trees and street lamps of the square. Nairn sat in a corner of the room, his face half concealed in darkness. By contrast, Sarah had placed the East German so that his face was well lit by a table lamp. Nairn examined the man's features as he spoke. He looked honest enough – but frightened.

'Was it really necessary to bring me over here? We could have talked in the café. I must be back at my friend's place in less than an hour, you know. We are all summoned to dinner by the head of the trade mission.'

'You can get a taxi outside,' snapped Nairn. 'But first I must get the facts clear. You are certain that your girlfriend wishes to leave her husband and come over as well, with her two children?'

'Quite certain.'

'But you are divorced – you will come alone?'

'We will come together.'

Nairn stretched back in his chair. 'I find it exceedingly odd that two privileged citizens of the German Democratic Republic – one with a mother who has given great service to the state and been honoured for it – should suddenly wish to risk the uncertainties of defection.'

The German winced. 'Then either you have never lived in the East or you are very short-sighted.'

'Am I?' Nairn's tone was cold, downright unfriendly.

Sarah poured them both beer from a can.

'We all grew up in England – I was born there and lived in your country until I was six. I *know* what we are missing.'

'But you are privileged people, with money, access to hard currency and special shops, weekend cottages in the country.'

52

'Yes – we have all that, but we want the freedom to think our own thoughts. You cannot know how important that is . . .'

'Something of a luxury, I should have thought. I suppose you also expect us to support you financially when you defect?'

Peter Werner flushed. 'We are hoping for some help at first, until we can get jobs.' A shadow of fear crossed his face. 'And because of our backgrounds we shall need protection. We shall be condemned as traitors, you must know that.'

'Ah yes, protection. Now, there's a problem. Defectors who need *protection* usually have something of value to offer, to justify the expense, you know . . . it is not cheap to protect lives for year after year.'

'But I have nothing to give except my science.' A note of desperation was creeping in. 'Surely you won't turn me away?'

'Probably not. I expect you'd get a permit to stay in Britain if you apply – though I can't guarantee it – if that's all you want.'

'I wish it *could* be, but I have difficult family connections. They will not let Geli and me live without interference. Unless we are helped and protected I think they . . . frankly, I think they might kill us. Like Georgi Markov . . . and there have been many others.'

Nairn puffed his pipe and eyed the younger man stonily. 'And after two meetings with Western security services in one week, they may shoot you anyway when you get back. Particularly if we leak your treachery to them.' Peter's face went grey. 'You do seem to have problems, Dr Werner.'

'But please, *please*,' the German was suddenly pleading. 'Why are you doing this to me? All I want is to live in the West; I can work to earn my living.'

Nairn looked up abruptly. 'Why do you call yourself "Werner"?'

'It is a surname sometimes used by my mother since she returned to the GDR. It seemed better for me to have a German name, now that I am an East German citizen.'

'And how *is* your mother these days?'

53

The sudden question seemed to throw Werner; he hesitated, but recovered quickly. 'She is in her late seventies, but fit and well.'

'She holds no official position now?'

'No. She is retired.'

'Is she well treated by the authorities?'

'She has received the Order of the Red Banner twice.'

'That is a Soviet decoration, not from the GDR – and she received it a long time ago. How is she being treated *now*?'

'Not as well as she might be.'

Nairn sighed. 'Could you be a little more frank with me, Dr Werner? I heard that she was almost an outcast, because of her upper-class background, because she is a Jew, because she has spoken out against repression?'

Peter looked shifty. 'I would not say that.'

'Well, what *would* you say, Dr Werner?' Nairn was suddenly shouting. 'Is she in danger – say, of being confined to a criminal asylum?'

'Of course not. How dare you suggest such a thing? She held responsible posts in the Party and the state, she gave her whole life to them.'

'She was a spy.'

'I told them that in San Francisco – I have kept nothing back.'

'But you promised valuable information, Dr Werner, and you do not seem to *have* any of that precious commodity . . . and let me ask you another simple question. How realistic are you to pretend that your mother will remain unmolested if you flee to the West? Has she no enemies? She could be treated very badly, very badly indeed.'

Peter did not meet Nairn's eyes. 'Yes, I know that. I wish to God it could be otherwise.'

'Yet you are still prepared to betray her!' Nairn snarled with contempt. 'I'm glad you are not my son.' He started to refill his pipe. 'The truth is that, despite a brilliant past, she's vulnerable, isn't she?'

The German nodded unhappily. 'I suppose she might be.'

'Rubbish,' roared Nairn. 'You know damn well that she is! To be safe she must defect herself. Well – *will* she defect?'

Werner looked as if he had been struck in the face. 'I – I haven't asked her. I don't know.'

'Then you had better take steps to find out.' Nairn stood up with an air of finality. 'You are asking a great deal of us, *Herr Doktor*. You want four of you, with nothing particular to offer, to be protected and supported for the rest of your miserable lives. Salaries, houses, cars, the lot.'

'I didn't ask for all that.'

'With your connections that's what it will bloody well come to. We will do it, but on one clear condition.'

'What is that?'

'That you bring your mother with you – and that she is willing to talk to us about the past. You owe it to her – and you owe it to us.'

The German looked aghast. 'But I cannot guarantee that!'

'Have to try hard then, won't you? Try *bloody hard*. Will a week be enough for you to talk to your mother?'

Werner sank his head into his hands. 'But I don't *want* to return to Berlin – my mother is not part of our plan. She will never leave Germany now and if I tell her of our plans, she may betray us.'

'I don't think so. She's still your mother. I don't believe she will be as willing to shop you as you are to betray her . . . and if she went to the authorities she'd be at risk herself.'

'God – I never thought it would be like this.'

'We live in hard times, Dr Werner. Now, after you are back in Berlin is there somewhere private you can meet one of us, away from your apartment? Preferably in the country?'

Peter hesitated. He wanted time to think, but was being railroaded. 'I suppose so . . . I have the use of a summer cottage in the south, near the Czech border.'

'Is it isolated?'

'Very – it stands by itself in a forest.'

'Then please arrange to meet my colleague there in ten days' time.' Nairn gestured towards Sarah, with a thin smile. 'Ingrid will be our courier. Good evening.' He rose abruptly, turned to the doorway and was gone.

Werner was left staring weakly at the closed door. He turned to Sarah with appealing eyes. 'For God's sake, who *is* that bastard? I thought you would welcome me – I'm already in terrible danger and I desperately need your help.'

She sat on the arm of his chair and stroked his face, acting out her role in Nairn's script. 'Don't worry, he's a hard man, but *I* know how you feel. We have to be cautious and I think he's testing that you're genuine. I'm sure we can work something out.'

11

London

Nairn and Simon mounted the steps under the white portico of the Athenaeum. Nairn had never joined a West End club, an ingrained streak of Quaker thrift making him reluctant to spend several hundred pounds a year on belonging to anything, but he was secretly a little flattered whenever Simon took him to his. They crossed the pillared entrance hall, a ticker-tape machine clattering in the corner, up the grand staircase to the first floor.

The long drawing room was empty and they sat in battered green leather armchairs by one of the marble fireplaces; the fire of artificial coals, fuelled by gas, threw out little heat. A waiter appeared discreetly and Simon ordered two gins with tonic.

'Thanks for your report,' he said to Nairn, when they were alone again. 'Very satisfactory so far. There's just one thing – can this girl of yours be trusted?'

'Of course she can – and so far I've handled most of it myself, without telling even Walker.'

'That's the best way, but I suppose we'll have to bring him in. You'll need intercepts, electronic surveillance, maybe watchers, won't you?'

The waiter brought their drinks, which to Nairn's surprise Simon paid for at once in cash. He lit his pipe and turned to face Simon. 'I'm not sure that I'll be wanting any of that.'

'You won't? How splendid!'

'I mean that, now I've made contact for you, I want out. Get somebody else to finish it off. Okay?'

Simon's eyes narrowed slightly, a little of the silver-haired urbanity slipping away. 'That's not very practical, David. What the devil's got into you?'

'I just don't like it. This chap Werner seems decent enough, so why not let him come over in the usual way? I don't care about Carteret enough to go through with blackmailing Werner, forcing him to put us in touch with his mother, trying to make her defect. It's bloody distasteful and it might all go wrong.'

'But Sonia is the key, dear boy. And we *must* have a solution to the problem; there's been penetration at the top, we must identify the traitor – or traitors.'

'Ay, it would be nice to know, right enough, but is it worth all this risk? Carteret's been dead thirteen years. If he was a traitor, he's doing no harm now.'

'Isn't he, David, *isn't* he? Good grief, barely a month passes without his name cropping up in the press – "*was the head of MI5 a traitor for a quarter of a century?*" There've been good, convincing books written about it. A security service in which no one has confidence is a national disaster. The Bettaney case didn't help, but I'm more troubled by who is there *now*.'

'Maybe nobody.'

'But even if the place is clean, it can't function in an atmosphere of perpetual suspicion, with everyone mistrusting everybody else.'

'You've got to be potty to join Box in the first place.'

Simon laughed. 'I suppose so, but you can't dismiss it like that, David. Every year or so suspicion falls on someone new, usually a man or woman who's given a lifetime of faithful service. Look at Brown – he spent a year under investigation.'

'He survived and became Director-General.'

'But it's unhealthy. It's *impossible*. How the devil can the thing operate if there's always a nagging suspicion that there's someone at the top working for Moscow? And that it's been going on for forty years?'

Nairn sank his gin and shrugged. 'Terrible, Jim, but it's your problem, not mine.'

'You could solve it. You *must* solve it if you're going to run the place.'

'But I'm not – no one's ever asked me, except you.'

'The PM wants you, David.'

'Does she, Jim? I doubt it. Anyway I'm fifty-eight, I've had a couple of lousy years with heart trouble and now I'm miraculously okay. I want to take it easy for a change, have a bit of fun before I drop dead.'

Simon stood up and walked to a window, studying the cars parked in Waterloo Place. It had started to rain and a taxi was drawing up below at the front door; two figures emerged, huddled under a black umbrella. The long room was still empty, but soon other members would be arriving for pre-dinner drinks.

'David, since Carteret died how many senior men and women have fallen under suspicion?'

'Heaven knows – I suppose six or seven.'

'There's a new one.'

'Really?' Nairn sounded bored. 'Who?'

'You know I can't tell you, David.'

'Why bring it up then?'

'Because it worries me. I don't believe there's a shred of truth this time, but a couple of ex-officers from Box 500 crawled out of the woodwork and put their views about. They went to Downing Street first and a private secretary saw them . . . they're coming to me next week. Officially I don't know yet.'

'Hard lines, Jim, but you get paid more than me for fielding that kind of thing.' Nairn fingered his empty glass meaningfully, but realized from Simon's basilisk stare that you got no second drink for non-co-operation. In the ensuing silence he picked up a thick red book lying on the wine table. It was *Who's Who* for 1968 and he turned to an entry, scanning it abstractedly: *Carteret, Sir Jack KBE CB* . . . Eventually he shot a glance at Simon. 'Is that it then? Can I go home to Chiswick?'

'I'm not leaving it there, David.' The beautifully modulated voice, still with a slight trace of Vienna, spoke quietly, almost threateningly. 'I want you to see this through. It's *vital* to close the file once and for all – and you can do it. It's in your own interests too.'

'Balls. It would be in my interests to take a long cruise with a nubile blonde. And don't bloody well tell me my country needs me. There are any number of young men in

59

Century House who'd take my job over tomorrow. It's worth thirty thousand a year and a K.'

'They won't get a K,' muttered Simon icily. 'That was personal to you and I'm beginning to wonder why we bothered. We'll leave it for now, but I'll ring you tomorrow. I want you to see this out – so think it over tonight. Will you?'

Outside the club, Nairn turned up his coat collar against the rain and hurried, head down, to Piccadilly Circus tube station. There he spent ten minutes in the only telephone box that had not been vandalized and caught a train to Acton Town. A young man was waiting for him in a pub a few hundred yards from the station. He stood up briskly as Nairn came in, wiping away a rivulet of rain-water running slowly down his forehead.

'Good evening, sir.'

'Why aren't you in Hereford, Colonel Thorne? Not that I'm anything but delighted to find you in Acton. Saved me a long drive.'

'I had to come up for a meeting at MOD, sir. What may I get you?'

'I'll do it, thanks – least I can do after dragging you out in this disgusting weather. What will it be?'

'A pint of Directors', please.'

They sat in a corner with two full tankards and Nairn sensed wetness in his right shoe. Damn it, he really must get that sole repaired. 'I have a problem, Colonel.'

'I hear you may have several, sir.'

Nairn eyed the young soldier with suspicion. 'And just *what* have you been hearing, Colonel?'

Thorne studied his beer as if hurt by Nairn's sharp tone. 'Oh, the usual gossip in the mess, sir. Probably nothing in it at all.'

'Just tell me, laddie, then I'll tell you what I had in mind.'

Thorne swallowed a long draught of beer. 'Well, one rumour going round is that you might be the next boss of Box 500, when that berk Alexander retires.'

'Uh-huh. But that's not all you've heard, is it?'

'Not quite, sir.'

'For Christ's sake, what else then?'

Thorne shifted awkwardly on the wooden bench, then spoke very fast. 'I was in Whitehall the other day and heard you were being blocked. Blackballed.'

'Blocked? By whom?'

'I don't know, but somehow it was all mixed up with Carteret. Some retired bloke had turned up from Canada . . .'

'Someone retired from the Security Service?'

'Where else? And he'd claimed it wasn't Carteret, or Brown or any of the others they've fingered over the years.'

'Who was it then?'

'He seemed to think it might be – look, I know it's bloody crazy – but he seemed to think it might be *you*, sir.'

Nairn looked stunned, then started to laugh. 'God, I sometimes think this business turns everyone who touches it insane. Some want me to run MI5, some say I'm a traitor. What utter balls!'

Thorne smiled weakly, but did not laugh. 'Glad you can take it like that, sir. Of course, I suppose you knew already . . . I thought you might be a bit upset. It's not a nice thing to happen, even though we all know it's rubbish.'

Nairn suppressed a mounting curiosity and tried to sound casual. 'It's the kind of daft thing that happens all the time, Thorne; one gets used to it. It's just a couple of loonies letting off steam.' He wished to God he knew who they were. 'Don't take it too seriously – if my outfit and Box had been penetrated to the extent some people think, we'd have a Marxist government in Downing Street by now.'

'I suppose so.' Thorne went to the bar to buy two more pints and, when he returned, Nairn changed the subject abruptly.

'Apart from all that, I *do* have a job for you, Colonel.'

'Fine.' They were back on reassuring ground, but the soldier hesitated. 'Just one thing, Sir David. This is *official*, isn't it? I mean, you're not – well, under investigation or anything?'

Nairn suppressed a burst of fury and laughed again. 'Bugger off, Jerry, this is straight from the co-ordinator himself and top priority. So let's get on with it, shall we?'

Thorne had come by car – a Range Rover – and dropped Nairn at his flat in Hartington Road fifteen minutes after they had left the pub. The older man climbed the concrete steps, opened the double-locked front door, poured a small malt whisky and flopped into an armchair by the window looking out over the river. Although it was dark he left the curtains undrawn, watching the red and green navigation lights of a police boat float past, before picking up the phone. Whatever was going on, he didn't like it.

Nairn spent nearly three hours on the phone before he went to bed, but was up at seven as usual. His driver came for him at eight and he spent the morning working in the office, leaving at eleven thirty, walking north over Westminster Bridge, to keep an appointment made the night before. By twelve he was on the terrace of the House of Commons, talking to a backbencher he had known for many years, a still comparatively young man of no apparent ambition but – or perhaps for that reason – close to the Prime Minister. He leant on the stone parapet, staring fixedly across the grey river, as Nairn listed his suspicions, systematically and without emotion.

'You know I can't say much, David, but you've got it mostly right. Nobody believes a word of it, of course.'

'Nobody?'

'Well, I suppose someone may be checking a few points. We can't totally ignore people like this, you know, and you've made a few enemies. Even people who've nothing against you think you behaved pretty oddly by helping that fellow in Vienna. The representative to the UN with the shady past – what was he called?'

'Cable. His daughter is in my office.'

'Good grief, is she? Is that wise?'

'I think so – she's very good.'

'On your head, David. But you certainly won't be taking over Five until all this is cleared up, you know.'

'I don't want to run the bloody place anyway, I've already told Simon that.'

'But they think you do, David, and *I* think you do. It's recognition, isn't it, even if you only stayed a few years? It's

62

your Order of the Red Banner. Look here, I don't believe a word of this stuff, nor does the PM, but somebody's bound to and, even if you don't take over from Alexander, you don't want to go under a cloud of suspicion, do you?'

'Does a bit of dirt peddled by malcontents matter so much?'

'You know it does. "No smoke . . ." they'll say. They always do.'

'Are you being straight with me? The PM really *does* take it as malicious gossip? Or am I going to wake up one morning like Carteret, summoned to South Audley Street like a criminal, to find a committee's been investigating behind my back for years?'

'If you were, I'd hardly tell you. But don't get uptight, David, you've been like a rock in shifting sands for a long time and we all damn well *know* we can trust you. This sort of thing is distasteful, but it's happened before, to equally innocent people.'

There was silence and they stood awkwardly side by side, staring at a swan bobbing on the water; then their eyes met. 'That's all I can say, but you've no stronger defender than Jim Simon. He's put his head on the block for you – that's why you should do what he wants, hit back by sorting it yourself. It wasn't you, Brown or Fell, or anyone like that. It was Carteret – and he probably left a successor, someone we've never found. Now there's a chance to settle it once and for all, so go and do it.'

'You're telling me it's my neck or Sonia's?'

'Not exactly, David.' Nairn wondered whether to believe him. 'Just help your friends to tell the malcontents where they can stuff their insinuations – see this job through.'

12

Devon

Sometimes Sarah hated David Nairn; sometimes she felt almost in love with him. Always she admired his intuitive brilliance as an intelligence officer. Brought up as the daughter of a none-too-successful diplomat, in her teens she had rejected the charade of embassy life and everything else to do with government service. But while she was trying to find a job and put some order into her chaotic life, Nairn had recruited her, in an autumn walk by the Thames at Chiswick, just outside a pub called the City Barge; and suddenly, at the age of twenty-one, she had found a way of life that fascinated her.

But it also had drawbacks; she turned back to the house, irritably kicking a groove in the yellow gravel. The grey stone of the Jacobean façade was ivy-clad and beautiful, but otherwise Edge was a pain. A draughty part-Victorian ruin, it was miles from any form of civilization and kept by curmudgeonly retainers. She associated it with humiliating training courses that showed how you'd last about ten minutes under cover in Warsaw, and with planning weekends of unparalleled boredom. This time it was the latter, but it was infuriating that Nairn had yet to tell her what they were planning, why or for whom.

As she crossed the hall, the flagstones seemed to radiate damp and cold; she wished that she had brought some warm trousers, not this silly blue dress with its high lace-trimmed neckline, suitable for VIP meetings. Nairn had been in the conference room for hours, poring over maps with men who looked like soldiers, despite their jeans and sweaters. He stuck his head out when he heard her footsteps clatter on the stone floor. 'Hello, Sarah.' He frowned. 'Is something the matter?'

'No. Is there anything I can do to help?' She put on a professional smile, biting back the fact that she was pissed off with him, Edge and the whole sodding weekend.

'Sorry you've had to hang about; I had to sort things out with the boys from Poole first, but I'd like to fill you in now.' About bloody time, she thought. 'Shall we go down by the lake?'

She had spent the last hour by the lake, but smiled icily: 'That would be nice.'

They strode around the patch of semi-stagnant water, its surface broken up by flat green leaves. At least Nairn was even taller than Sarah, so she did not have to mince along as with shorter men. 'You know about Carteret and Fell?' he asked abruptly.

'I know about Sir Jack Carteret and all the rumours about him being a Soviet spy while running MI5 back in the sixties. But who was Fell?'

'Richard Fell was his deputy. He was in Box for about thirty years – like Carteret – but retired a few years before him. Carteret survived by throwing suspicion on Fell – the poor bastard was crucified. He's been living on in disgrace for twenty years.'

'I didn't know that, David.' He had told her to stop calling him 'Sir David' when she went to work in his support staff, but it still seemed vaguely unnatural to be on first name terms with the Chief's deputy. 'I also don't know why we're here. Are you ever going to tell me?'

'Of course.' He smiled vaguely and his stride quickened. 'I suppose it goes back to 1917 . . . I suspect the Soviets have seen us as hostile ever since Reilly organized that abortive coup in Moscow in 1918 – what the Russians call the Lockhart Plot, though I doubt Lockhart had much to do with it. But, although it seems barmy now, it *was* meant to destroy their revolution and unfortunately it coincided with Dora Kaplan's attempt to assassinate Lenin – he never fully recovered from the bullet wounds, you know.'

'David,' she ground her teeth with impatience. 'Exactly *what* has this got to do with anything?'

'I've always thought it might be why they've taken so

much trouble to penetrate our security and intelligence services, don't you? We've always been a special Soviet target – and we do seem to have collected more than our fair share of traitors. Burgess, Maclean, Philby, Blunt, Cairncross, Long, the list goes on for ever.'

'It all seems a long time ago and if we walk round this bloody pond again I'm going to get dizzy.' They sat on a bench and Nairn turned to face her, the glint of battle in his eyes.

'Ah, but it's still going on, there's the rub. All through the fifties and early sixties most Soviet defectors went to America, claiming they were afraid to come to us because there was a high-level traitor in Five or Six, or both. And Five was a complete disaster – failure after failure. Burgess and Maclean scarpered, and attention focused on Philby. By 1962 there was a massive case against him and Carteret decided that Philby should be confronted in Beirut and offered immunity from prosecution in exchange for a full confession – for co-operation in bringing the ring to an end. But Philby *knew* that this was going to happen long beforehand. There was time for Yuri Modin, his Russian case officer, to visit Beirut and make a plan with him. Philby pretended to co-operate, but gave nothing away – then quietly vanished on a Soviet freighter and surfaced in Moscow. The rest you know. It was a complete cock-up on our side.'

'Okay, but so what?'

'So who told the Russians and allowed Philby to escape? There was a post-mortem and it was clear that only five people, all in MI5, knew what was going to happen – Carteret, as Director-General, Fell, two other officers and a secretary. It seemed pretty clear that it couldn't be one of the three junior staff – none of them had ever done anything suspect in their entire lives and they didn't have the necessary access anyway. One of the two officers, Embling, had been studying the long line of security failures since the war, the way the Russians had bust the atom bomb programme and every other major advance in defence, the Soviet agents allowed to escape – above all the way defectors had avoided London like the plague. Many defectors to America had claimed there was a high-level mole in MI5 and, after the shambles over Philby, Embling was certain that it had to be Carteret or Fell, probably Carteret. He was so appalled that he went to Stephen Black, who'd run Box for three years before becoming head of our service, and asked him what to do.'

'What happened then?'

'The fuss went on for years – it's still going on now. The earlier moles – even Philby – had never got right to the *top* of one of our services; they'd been flawed characters, drunks and queers, mostly with the same Cambridge background, often only in a post for a few years. Carteret and Fell were different. They weren't gay, they'd both been to Oxford, they were a couple of dullish blokes who'd been in Five since before the war, thirty years or more, and ended up at the very top. If one of *them* was a spy, with perfect scope for leaving successors behind him, Christ – Moscow really had taken us to the cleaners. There were ghastly, traumatic investigations; Five's whole credibility collapsed and was never recovered. No government's trusted it since. Worse, neither of them was cleared, neither of them confessed.

'Carteret turned the heat on Fell, who retired early. He's been living out in Buckinghamshire as a recluse, surrounded by suspicion, for more than twenty years. If he was innocent he was treated pretty badly. Appallingly. Then they investigated Carteret, but he died before anything could be proved.'

'Does it matter?'

'Yes, it matters like hell. Five might as well be closed down unless we can sort this out – and we do *need* it, or something like it, in a time of terrorism and subversion. And if Carteret was an agent, how many others did he leave behind? Who's the top traitor in Five *now*? That's what we have to know.'

'And where does Sonia fit in?'

'She was in Oxford during the war, when Five was evacuated to Blenheim Palace. We believe she ran the traitor then – his code-name was "Alec". Carteret and Fell were both at Blenheim at the time.'

'But I've read the files, David. Sonia was a lifetime Soviet agent, they gave her the Order of the Red Banner, and she's nearly eighty! Why the hell should *she* help you?'

'Maybe she won't, Sarah, maybe she won't, but one of her sons is in the process of defecting – and that makes her vulnerable. Everything she did in the past won't matter when Peter goes – she'll be suspect. She's made enemies over there and they'll kick her out of the Party, disgrace her, take away her home. She'll be in danger, real danger, and if we offer a helping hand their rejection might just break her will to resist.'

13

Thüringer Wald

At first the prospect of going East under a false identity had terrified Sarah, but now that she was there she felt confident – almost elated by the challenge – as the Volkswagen Golf hummed along the highway towards the East German frontier.

After three days at Edge, with Nairn summoning a stream of people from a bewildering variety of departments and obscure corners of Special Forces, she had finally flown off to Rome, then to Istanbul and back to Vienna. Her passport was Austrian and described her as Ingrid Ruckenbauer, born in Linz, 17 November, 1962. She had hired the little green car in Vienna, where she had applied for legitimate visas to visit Czechoslovakia and East Germany. That had taken several days, but eventually she had set off down the autobahn to Linz, where she had turned north, across the Danube, to cross the Czech border at Wullowitz.

The police on the Austrian side of the frontier had examined her passport cursorily, smiling good-naturedly in their baggy green uniforms. That had been the easy part: the hundred yards to the Czech frontier post had seemed interminable and she had gone tense inside when the Czech guard took her passport and visas away to a hut for examination. But then he had returned, sub-machine gun still tucked under his arm, and waved her on without a word. She had driven through the rolling forests of Czechoslovakia without problem, stopping the night at a tourist hotel fifty miles beyond Prague.

Now the second frontier was close and she was no longer afraid. It had started to rain heavily and Sarah could not imagine border guards between two Warsaw Pact states being too assiduous if it meant getting wet. Once over the border, her Austrian identity should work easily. Mostly she would pass as a native, with her command of the language, blonde hair and Saxon appearance; but if challenged she would be an Austrian on holiday to avoid the danger of using false East German documents. The sky grew black and rain lashed the windscreen as the road descended from Chomutov.

The frontier crossing was more worrying than she had expected. On both sides young men in military capes, dripping with rain, pored officiously over her papers and on the East German side the guard eyed her Viennese licence plate with distaste. 'What is your destination in the Democratic Republic?' he barked; he must have been born years after the war, but sounded like a throw-back to the SS. Two others, rain or no rain, shoved long-handled mirrors on wheels under the car.

'I'm going to Karl-Marx-Stadt, then touring in Thüringer Wald.'

'And what is the purpose of your journey, Fraulein Ruckenbauer?'

'I am on holiday.'

He waved her on brusquely. 'Then be careful to observe all traffic signs and not to leave litter by the road or in camping places!'

She drove westwards, first on the autobahn, then along dusty roads that seemed left behind from the 1930s. Sarah passed long, dark farmhouses with high-pitched roofs and occasional buildings – a post office or an electricity sub-station – in the harsh concrete style of the Nazi period. She was in the centre of Europe, but there was little sign of the armies that had thundered back and forth across it forty and fifty years before.

Early in the afternoon she found the rough track, as described by Peter, and the car bounced up it for about a mile, dense forest to either side. The hut stood in a clearing, with a view to mountains in the distance. It was more like a log cabin than a hunting lodge, but it had a steeply sloping wood-shingled roof with dormer windows; there was a small balcony above the front door. A Mercedes was parked in an outbuilding and a stream bubbled over a bed of pebbles, forming a small pool not far from the house.

Sarah had half feared that Peter would lose his nerve and not turn up – or even betray her. But there was no sign of waiting Vopos and there he was, opening the door and coming out to greet her. Soon she would know whether Sonia was coming quietly, or with difficulty, or not at all.

The attic of the apartment block in East Berlin was dusty and the man in blue overalls sneezed as he knelt by the low window. His municipal repair services card and a few West German ten-mark notes had worked wonders with the *Hausbesorger*, who assumed that anyone handing out hard currency must be from the security police. Swiftly he pulled out his wallet of tools and selected a hole, through which one could see daylight, where the roof tiles came down to the attic floor. He enlarged it and rested the tiny transmitter in the space between the joists where the floorboards ended. The directional microphone was like a thin knitting needle and he thrust it through the hole, using a small eye-glass to line it up on the window of the apartment opposite, then stapled it into place on the rough wood of a rafter. He checked the signal by plugging in an earpiece and fiddled with the device until he was satisfied. From now on it would transmit direct to a tape-recorder in the Embassy.

Back on the concrete stairs, he brushed the dust from his overalls and hurried down to the empty apartment of the professor of law, who, he had told the caretaker, was a suspect person and the object of his visit.

Sarah parked the Golf in the barn and walked back to the wooden cabin. They sat in the kitchen, an old cast iron stove belching smoke in the corner, and Peter poured two glasses of schnapps. 'The stove will stop smoking soon.' He forced a wry grin. 'The chimney gets damp when the place is shut up for weeks on end.'

'It's a beautiful spot – is the cottage yours?'

He shook his head. 'No. I do have a summer house, nearer to Berlin, but this belongs to a friend of mine. I use it from

71

time to time. It is a very isolated spot, so I hope we shall be safe here.'

'Does anyone know where you are?'

'No one. I mentioned to a few friends that I was going to the country for the weekend, to cover my absence, but I did not say where.'

'Good. Now, have you seen your mother?'

'Yes,' he glanced up bitterly from his schnapps. 'I did what your bloody friend ordered.'

Sarah ignored the jibe. 'And what was the result?'

'She was very angry – angry and frightened. She said it would be madness and disloyal for Geli and me to defect – that she will not come with us.'

Sarah smiled reassuringly. 'One would expect her to react in that way at first.'

'I think she was quite definite – I warned your Scottish colleague of that in Brussels.' He glared at her with a mixture of fear and fury in his eyes. 'So you have made me show my hand – and for what? Now I'm in terrible danger and people like you have no conception of the suffering the state can inflict in a country like this.' He spat the words at her. 'So get me out, for God's sake, and quickly – you owe me that, at least.'

'Of course we will . . . but are you *sure* she was so definite? I know your mother's a lifelong Marxist, but she must realize that she'll be in danger if you and Geli scarper. Past loyalty and service won't save her. Doesn't she understand that?'

'How the hell should I know?' Peter's receding hairline glistened with tiny beads of sweat and his smooth face reddened. He was almost shouting. 'Just stop playing with me and get me out. If you've brought the false papers you promised, I can reach the frontier within an hour.'

Sarah felt a surge of contempt. His combination of self-pity and callous indifference was sickening, but she bit her feelings back. 'Be realistic, Peter,' she said evenly. 'We aren't amateurs and I didn't cross the border carrying phoney documents with your photograph on them. I might have been stopped and searched – and then what sort of mess would you be in? They were sent to our Embassy in East Berlin by diplomatic bag and we've arranged for you to pick them up at a drop.' She poured more schnapps and stared pensively through the window. The sun had come out and the silver water of the stream looked more inviting than the stifling, smoky kitchen. 'You'll be all right, so for Christ's sake calm down. But we want your mother, too – isn't she just a little ambivalent?'

He scowled and shrugged. 'I've no idea. She's been disappointed by the way things have turned out politically in the last ten or twenty years and she's made herself unpopular with some of the hard-liners in the Party. She's spoken out against repression – she's Jewish you know – and they've all forgotten what she did in the war. She's been attacked in spiteful little ways: losing access to special shops, having to move out of the best residential areas, into a smaller apartment, that kind of thing . . .'

'She was a woman of great courage – she deserves better than that. But when you go her enemies will be off the leash – they'll crucify her. Can you just sit back in a comfortable safe house in England or America and watch it happen?'

'No – I should much prefer it if she came too, with my father, but I can't persuade her. You will have to do that.'

God, you're a shit, she thought; but she knew the time had come for another approach. 'I'm going for a swim in that pool,' she said abruptly. 'Will you come too?'

'No, thank you – the water is too cold.'

Sarah slipped out of her clothes in the kitchen and draped a towel round her shoulders; it was just about long enough to cover her slim buttocks. With long, firm thighs and flaxen hair, she looked like a Wagnerian goddess or pure Aryan SS call-girl. She walked barefoot across the grass to the rock pool, swaying her hips and dropping the towel after a few yards so that he would get an eyeful of her naked. At the edge of the water she turned, pushing her breasts out, and waved at him cheekily. He was looking away at the mountains, lost in thought.

Sod it, she thought – perhaps the bloody man was gay, or just too terrified to care. She bent forward, dived and gasped in shock as she hit the water. It was so icy that it was painful. She kicked a few angry strokes before giving up and climbing

73

out to dry in the sun; but then, from the corner of her eye, she noticed him approaching.

Late in the afternoon they walked through the forest, emerging on a plateau covered in heather and yellow gorse bushes. Below them a road meandered along the bottom of a deep valley. Suddenly Peter started and fell to the ground, pulling Sarah after him. Cautiously they raised their heads and peered through the bushes.

'Look,' he sounded scared and clutched her arm so tightly that it was painful. 'That grey car.' It was parked off the road and the blue lamp and Volkspolizei sign were clearly visible. 'What the devil are *they* doing here?'

Sarah felt a wave of fear too, but was determined to stay calm. 'Surely it's just a routine patrol: they come up here sometimes, don't they?'

'Not often. I don't like it – could something have leaked in London?'

'Not a chance,' she grinned at him with more conviction than she felt. 'But let's get back into the wood so they don't see us.' She wriggled round on her stomach, trying to avoid the spiky bushes, and started to crawl back to the trees.

At the cabin nothing had been disturbed. She found some pork schnitzels and frozen chips in the kitchen freezer; and they ate sitting in front of a log fire, with a bottle of Bulgarian red wine. 'Forget about the Vopos, Peter.' Sarah stood up and stroked his face gently. 'We're doing nothing suspicious.'

He groaned. 'I have already committed high treason – and how the hell am I supposed to explain you away if they turn up to check the house?'

'Easy – I'm an Austrian tourist and you picked me up for a screw. Is that so unusual?'

'I suppose not.' His face was in darkness, but the greenish-yellow light from the flames flickered weirdly on his bare neck and arms.

'Let's go back to your mother. Isn't there *anything* you know that would help me?'

'Not much. But I was thinking when we were out in the forest, trying to remember – she *must* be more ambivalent than she seems. I don't know my mother all that well and

74

I'm not sure that anyone ever has, at least not since she was in her twenties . . . but I do know that there were two occasions when she felt betrayed by the Party.'

'Betrayed? How?'

'Don't misunderstand me. Both times she found her faith again, but they shook her badly and made her very unhappy.'

'Tell me about them.'

'The first was in Shanghai, in 1932 . . .'

14

Shanghai – 1932

It was 17 December, grey and wet outside. Ruth spent the morning alone in the house, playing with Micha, but inwardly she felt listless and depressed. She had not seen Richard for several days and there had been no reply when she telephoned his apartment. Then Grischa, a German she barely knew, had rung saying that Richard was at Grischa's house and wanted to talk to her there. Crossly she had ignored this to pay him out – let bloody Richard ring her himself, she was not a concubine.

Late in the afternoon she had met Rolf in the city and they had gone to a dreary meeting of the East Asia Society in a room over the China Institute. The son of a German missionary had talked maddeningly about China three thousand years ago, apparently oblivious to the revolution going on around them now, then a teacher called Kuck had shown lantern-slides of his visit to Shansi and Kansu. Afterwards Rolf had asked them all back for supper and now they sat in the dining room, stolidly making conversation while she was run off her feet feeding and watering them.

The telephone rang and the room fell silent. It stood on a desk in the alcove behind a curtain of hanging bamboo and Ruth pushed this aside to pick up the receiver. On the wall was a picture of white hoar-frost hovering over a small lake, the Schlachter See on the edge of Berlin. 'It's me – Richard,' said the familiar voice, vibrant with life. 'I've been waiting all afternoon for you to call me.'

She turned her back on the crowd of silent guests, embarrassed not to be alone, and spoke in a whisper. 'I'm so sorry, darling. I had to go to a meeting and then they all came back here for something to eat.'

'Are they still there?'

'Yes.'

'Never mind, but Ruth, this is urgent. I have been ordered to go on a journey. At once – tonight. It was quite unexpected. I'm sorry.'

She sat down in the chair by the desk, Richard's chair, reeling with shock, and tried to understand. 'For how long?' She knew better than to ask where to. 'When will you be back?'

'I'm not coming back.'

'But Richard, then I must *see* you. Where are you? Can I come now . . . please?' Her voice trembled and suddenly she was weeping, instinctively aware that something terrible and final was happening. 'Please, Richard?' She stole a glance into the room through her mist of tears. Fortunately the desultory conversation seemed to have begun again.

'Ruth, my love, you must stay where you are or you will attract suspicion. You cannot tell them all "I am going to see my lover who is also . . ."' he chuckled. 'Are you sitting on my chair by the desk?'

'Yes, darling.'

'Good. Then say goodbye to it for me.'

'But Richard –' She wanted to wipe the tears from her cheeks but maddeningly both her hands were occupied with the earpiece and the pedestal of the telephone. She could not think clearly. 'What on earth is going on? You must be coming back some time. *Aren't* you? We *will* be together again . . . in a month or two . . . won't we, Richard?'

He did not reply for a moment, then faltered. 'I hope so, but for now I must go away. Ruth –' His voice caught and she knew the truth. 'Thank you. Thank you for everything. You've been wonderful, I *love* you and I shall never, *never* forget. From now on you will be Sonia and you will carry great responsibility. You will hear soon. Keep faith, my love . . . *alles, alles Gute, Ruth, und Auf Wiedersehen.*'

He was gone and she was left wiping her eyes, hoping the others would not see that she had been weeping. Two minutes ago she had been so happy. Richard, her secret love, so precious despite – perhaps because – she would never dance with him in public, never bear his child. Two

77

short years of joy and now he was going away – she sensed that it was to Moscow. The dream was shattered and she felt this cruel, heartbreaking premonition that she would never see him again. She sat hunched in the chair, where he had sat so often, and fought to put a brave face on it. She could weep tomorrow, she could weep for the rest of her life, but now she must be a silly German *Hausfrau*. She pushed back through the rattling bamboo and went to fetch some wine from the kitchen.

Sarah slept fitfully in one of the three bedrooms, woken up frequently by the noise of Peter moving about and flushing the old-fashioned lavatory, turning her new insight into Sonia over and over in her mind. In the morning Peter was moody and uptight as they breakfasted on coffee and coarse rye bread, but soon they were sitting by the stream and talking again. 'What happened after Richard Sorge left Shanghai?' she asked.

Peter lit a cigarette, exhaling the smoke into the clean mountain air. 'After a time my mother was summoned for the first time to Moscow for training. Her first husband, Rolf, had also become an agent, so he arranged for her to leave Michael with his grandparents in Czechoslovakia. My brother could not be taken to Moscow because, at that age, he would inevitably have learnt to speak a little Russian – which he might then blurt out in another country and attract suspicion. Then Sonia went back east, for liaison work with Communist partisans fighting the Japanese in Manchuria. My sister, Nina, was born there, in Mukden. After two years mother returned to Moscow through a Germany in which Hitler had come to power, horrified by the sight of Jews scrubbing the streets, lashed by Brownshirts with bull-whips. The windows of Jewish businesses had been smashed and Jews were already disappearing in *Nacht und Nebel* to the first concentration camp at Dachau north of Munich. Even travelling through the country under a false name she wished for less semitic features and felt terrifyingly at risk. Her own family – grandfather, grandmother, her four sisters, brother Jurgen and his wife – had all fled from Berlin to London.

'After two years in Poland my mother was awarded the

Order of the Red Banner, the highest decoration of the Red Army, promoted to major and sent to Switzerland. She was secretly very proud of her Red Banner, although she was ordered to leave the incriminating insignia behind in Moscow. In Montreux she was made a lieutenant-colonel and in 1940, ordered to marry Len, so that she could get a British passport, and travel to England.'

An hour later Sarah was still following Sonia's story through the Second World War. 'But, Peter,' she cried in desperation. 'When was the *second* betrayal you mentioned?'

'Oh, that? Like the first it concerned Richard Sorge. He is my mother's only weakness, you know. Through him she is still vulnerable, for she loved him even more than her Marxism.'

'Tell me.'

'It was in the late summer of 1946. She went to meet her contact from the Soviet Embassy, at Brompton Cemetery in London.'

At the end of their discussion, Sergei hesitated, as if about to break the rules in some way. 'Sonia?' She smiled at him and he responded abruptly. 'Did you know that Sorge is dead?'

It was like a vicious kick in the stomach and she reeled, clinging to his arm until she was sitting on a broken-down tomb. 'No. Oh God, *no* – I thought he was still in the Far East.' It did not occur to her to ask why Sergei should have expected her to be interested.

'They arrested him in Japan in 1942.' Sergei sat with his arm round her shoulder and spoke very fast. 'He was betrayed. I don't think he was badly treated by them, but they hanged him in Tokyo, in the prison at Sugamo, on 7 November, 1944.' He paused gravely. 'The twenty-seventh anniversary of the Bolshevik Revolution. I am sorry.'

She did not weep, but sat staring blindly into the trees. Almost all the while she had been in Oxford, poor Richard had been in prison. He had died alone and for two years she had not even known it. 'Thank you for telling me,' she said, watching as the Russian walked away through the gate into

Brompton Road. When he was out of sight she let the tears come and dashed into a thicket of trees, where she broke down with great, ugly snorting sobs, leaning forward to grip a lichened trunk with both hands, her head hanging down like a runner at the end of a marathon.

When the sobbing stopped, she stayed in the cemetery, still weeping silently as she walked the empty paths, her whole body aching with grief. She also felt waves of anger – perhaps they had been right not to tell her of his arrest when she was under the pressure of running Fuchs, but they had kept his death from her for two whole years. It was inhuman and she had never felt such fury with the Centre before.

After a time she left and paused outside the gates. A flower-seller had a stall on the pavement and she bought a small bunch of red roses, at the price of nearly six shillings. Sonia went back into the cemetery, clutching them like a sleepwalker, and turned right down a gravel path, suddenly aware that there was no grave on which she could lay them.

A week later she cycled out to make her monthly pick-up from the drop on the Oxford–Banbury road. Leaning her bicycle against the tree, she checked that no one was passing and knelt to feel under the root. There was nothing there. She stood up, puzzled; it was conceivable that they had nothing for her, but it had never happened before.

The same thing happened next month and she decided to use the emergency telephone number Sergei had given her. There was a red phone box a mile down the road from the drop, so she dialled the operator and asked for the Kensington number.

'Place one shilling in the slot, caller, and press button A when they answer.' But there was no ringing tone, just a hollow whine. 'I'm sorry, caller, the line appears to be out of order.'

'But my call is very urgent, a matter of life and death. Could you try again? *Please?*'

'Certainly, caller.' There was silence for two or three minutes, punctuated by clicks and buzzes, then the woman's voice came back. 'I'm sorry, caller, but the number you gave me has been disconnected. Press button B to retrieve your money.'

'I see. Thank you.' So that was it – the Centre had stopped communicating with her. She must not approach them: that was the inviolable rule and if she tried they would ignore her. It was the end – and there could only be one reason. She was threatened with exposure.

Suddenly, standing outside the phone box, she felt desolate, alone, and very, very frightened. Sorge was dead and the Centre had no more use for her. In a few short weeks they had destroyed the two great commitments of her life. The only agent she had was Alec and his drop was already empty: she must never contact him again. She was cut off in a hostile country where every policeman, every soldier was an enemy – and how long could she last, without money, without help from the Centre? What would they do to her when they caught her? Her face was harrowed but rigid as she pedalled back to the cottage.

15

London

Nairn was puzzled. Every day he received a sealed envelope from Cheltenham of intercepts arising from keywords he had defined himself, for the small number of cases he was handling direct. This Tuesday there had been fifteen flimsies, fourteen of which simply filled in gaps as he had expected, but one which did not make sense. It was a signal from the Soviet Mission to the United Nations in New York, but its text was in German and it was addressed to the Ministry for State Security in East Berlin. It was in a new code and only parts had been deciphered, but Peter Werner's name occurred several times.

Not for the first time, he had an uneasy feeling about the cold, pale-eyed German; and was troubled for Sarah's safety. That girl had courage and brains – he had great respect for her as an intelligence officer, but he had never intended to place her in serious danger. With a worried frown he called his secretary on the intercom. 'Two calls, please, Jean – both scrambler, immediate. Get me Charlton at the embassy in East Berlin first, then the duty officer at our place in the West.'

'But why didn't she get out?' demanded Sarah. 'Christ, it must have been *awful*, alone in a country where you risked jail or death for espionage, cut off by the only people who could help you!'

'She had no money, no visas for Berlin – and where else could she go?' Peter shrugged dismissively. 'Germany was in ruins and occupied. In any case travel was soon impossible, for within a month England was in the grip of the worst

82

winter for a hundred years. It snowed for weeks and, although I was only three, I remember the cottage being bitterly cold. Mother could keep only the kitchen range going with wood and coal – there was no heat in the other rooms, which were freezing. We had no electricity because of the power cuts, just smoking oil-lamps, and we were always hungry. Because we were German the villagers would not help us.'

Bring out the violins, thought Sarah, irritated by the hint of self-pity that kept surfacing in Peter. 'And all the time she feared they might come to arrest her?'

'I suppose so, but we children knew nothing of that.'

'But it was a false alarm, wasn't it?' asked Sarah bluntly. 'Didn't the Centre reactivate her after about six months?' He stared at her in silence. 'Klaus Fuchs came back to Harwell in June 1946 and she was running him again in less than a year, *wasn't* she?'

'I really have no idea when it started again.'

'But it *did* start again?'

'Oh yes. She ran Fuchs until we left England.'

'When did your father come back from Germany?'

'Early in 1947. Life got back to normal and in June my grandparents came to stay for a holiday in the countryside. Grandmother had a heart attack and mother rushed for the doctor. The only telephone in the village was out of order and she had to cycle into the town. The doctor brought her back in his car, but it was too late; grandmother had died. We buried her in the village churchyard. Grandfather was very upset – and he stayed on with us at Great Rollright, instead of going back to the empty flat in London.'

'How long did he stay?'

'I think until October. He fell ill and went back to London – into hospital. He had cancer. Mother went to see him often and he lived until 25 November. They say he died very peacefully and he was buried in the churchyard, in the same grave as his wife. Mother loved them both deeply, you know; it was a terrible year for her.'

'Was your grandfather still there when MI5 sent investigators to Great Rollright?'

Peter looked at her shiftily. 'So you know about that, do you? Yes, they came in August or September of 1947.'

'What happened?'

16

Great Rollright – 1947

There was a hammering on the door in the middle of the afternoon. Three men stood outside in the yard, all in civilian clothes. 'I am a police officer,' said one, displaying his warrant card. 'May we come in?'

Sonia recovered quickly from her shock. 'Would you like a cup of tea?' She ushered them into the flagstoned kitchen where her father was sitting at the table reading. Len was outside, digging in the garden.

'Thank you – but first I must raise a serious question with you. Are you Mrs Ursula Beurton?'

'I am.' She filled a kettle and placed it on the black iron of the kitchen range.

'Then we have reason to believe that you are married bigamously.'

She almost burst out laughing in relief, but reacted as if offended. 'Of course not, that is a most insulting suggestion. I have been married before and divorced in order to marry my present husband.'

'When were you divorced, and where?'

'In 1940, in Switzerland, where I was living at the time.'

'Do you have documents to prove this?'

'Yes, but it may take a little time to find them.'

'We shall wish to see them before we leave.'

'In the meantime,' one of the other men interrupted abruptly, 'there is something else. We know that for many years you were a Russian agent.' Sonia swayed as she felt the tight dryness of fear in her throat, but said nothing, pressing her hands on the table in case they trembled. These two must be from MI5. Her father went on reading as if he could not hear.

The man who had accused her studied her face sternly before he spoke again. 'However we believe that you ceased to be active after the Soviet Union invaded Finland and have not spied here in England. In fact, we have come to ask whether you might be able to help us in certain ways.'

Sonia wondered how much they really knew, with a nagging fear that in some way they were tricking her; or were they just out to scare her with a bigamy charge, then ask for co-operation to forget it? 'I will make some tea.' She bustled into the kitchen, calling over her shoulder, 'and find those papers.'

'Also call your husband, please.'

Len came in and sat down with them at the table while Sonia poured tea, her father still reading as if nothing untoward were happening. 'Do you want me to go out while you question my husband?'

'No need for that,' the officer smiled knowingly. 'On the whole I'd sooner you stayed here where we can see you.' He turned to Len. The other man from MI5 was taking notes. 'Mr Beurton, we believe you were a friend of Alexander, sometimes known as Allen, Foote?'

'Footie? Yes, I knew him a long time ago – what's he up to now?' Len did not mention Switzerland. They had been warned that Foote, their fellow agent who had stayed in Switzerland, had recently defected back to Britain, but they did not know whether he had given the authorities evidence against them.

'You knew Foote in Montreux, I think?' The question was addressed to Len. 'What were you doing there?'

'Living and working.' Len answered shortly, making it clear that he was not keen to say any more.

'And you?' The officer turned to Sonia.

'The same.'

'Not a Soviet agent, working against our common enemy, the Nazis?'

Sonia evaded the question. 'I have not been an agent of any kind since I became a British subject by marrying my husband. I have been completely loyal to Britain.'

The discussion continued nebulously, with Sonia making fresh tea and repeatedly stressing her loyalty to Britain. One of the MI5 men made an effort to be friendly and admired the cottage. 'I should like to live in a pretty village like this.'

'Perhaps I could rent you a room?' Sonia's joke did nothing to lighten the strained atmosphere. The visitors again raised the question of co-operation, without being specific, but after a couple of hours they left, saying that they would return in a few days.

'What happened then?' asked Sarah, pouring the last of the Bulgarian wine.

'I remember very clearly. My mother was terrified, absolutely terrified, and left the cottage on father's motor-cycle an hour after the MI5 men had left.'

'Could your mother *ride* a motorbike?'

'Oh yes – she learnt in China.'

'Where did she go?'

'She did not come back until next day – I suppose she went to London.'

'And how quickly did the men from MI5 come back?'

'They never came back at all. We never saw them again.'

'They *never* came back?' Sarah remembered the dusty files she had seen in Century House. It just did not tally.

'No, never.'

'And these men didn't search the house?'

'No. If they had I suppose they'd have found the radio. That was always a weak point.'

'How odd – and how soon after this did you all flee to East Berlin?'

'Flee?'

'I thought you all went "on holiday" to Berlin a month or so later and never came back?'

'Oh no.' Peter's surprise was clearly genuine. 'We stayed another two and a half years.'

'Another two and a half *years*? You mean your mother didn't leave *and* she wasn't arrested? She must have become a double agent?'

'Good Lord no.'

'Peter – it just doesn't make *sense*.' All the files said Sonia had left in 1947; if she had stayed until 1950, something didn't fit. Sarah wondered how quickly she could get a message for Nairn to the embassy in East Berlin. Aloud she said: 'Do you mean she also went on running Fuchs after 1947, even after the visit from MI5?'

'Oh yes, he came to the cottage a few times. So far as I know she ran Klaus Fuchs until February 1950.'

They sat up late talking while Peter finished another bottle of wine and became pie-eyed. Next morning he had a hangover and she made a large pot of black coffee.

'I'm going to Berlin now, to see your mother.' She spread a street plan of East Berlin on the kitchen table and pointed to the green patch of a park. 'There's a crack in a flight of concrete steps here, near to the lake, not far from a sausage stand which is closed in the evening. Your exit papers will be there for collection as from tomorrow. There is a West German passport in the name of Weinlander, with the correct visas for a visit to this country and to Czechoslovakia.'

'Why Czechoslovakia?'

'It is too risky for you to try to cross into West Berlin. You must drive south into Czechoslovakia and cross into Austria. No one will be looking for you on that route.' He nodded, slowly sipping coffee with bloodshot eyes. 'Now, this is important, Peter. Your visas are for a journey *into* East Germany from West Berlin, through the country and *out* to Czechoslovakia. They don't allow you to go back to West Berlin, so for Christ's sake don't try.'

Sarah explained how he would receive a coded phone call when his mother was due to leave. 'A woman will phone and ask if you are Dr Kocian, the paediatrician. Treat it as a wrong number. That is the signal – don't try to go before then, sunshine, or you'll blow the whole thing.' Sarah kissed him goodbye, drove down the rutted forest track back to the road, and turned north.

At the first crossroads an unmarked car fell in behind her and she could see in the mirror that its occupants were two men in leather jackets. They had to be police, but she suppressed her panic and maintained a steady fifty. If they knew who she was, there was nothing to be done; if they were just suspicious, she was confident that she could bluff her way out. After about five miles, the car turned off and Sarah was left untroubled all the rest of the way to Berlin.

17

Great Rollright – 1950

January in the low hills of north Oxfordshire was cold, but nothing like the blizzards two years ago, in the winter of 1947. The Firs had become a comfortable home and the children had grown to love the cottage. Micha was now nearly nineteen and had won a scholarship to Aberdeen University, where he was studying philosophy, but the other two were delighted to have Len at home all the time, his leg still in plaster after a motor-cycle accident last October. It was late in the evening and rain beat noisily on the windows. Sonia was alone by the wood-burning stove in the living room, curled in an armchair reading, drowsy in the heat, with Len and the children asleep upstairs.

He came in silently from the kitchen, where the door to the yard was not locked. She did not notice him at first, then turned to see the black figure in the doorway and started in terror. 'Who are you?' she cried. 'How dare you come into my house like that!'

He took off his dripping hat. 'Don't shout – you'll wake the others. It's me, Alec.' He wiped rain from his face with a handkerchief. 'I'm sorry I've brought so much water in with me – I parked the car a long way down the road, in a wood, and walked back.'

She sprang up. 'But you shouldn't be here! It's forbidden – and dangerous. How did you know where I lived?'

'It's on your file, of course. I've been protecting you these last two years, otherwise you'd be in jail. Didn't you realize that?' He sneezed violently.

Stunned by the revelation, Sonia did not respond.

'You don't have any whisky, do you?' He sneezed again, laying his soaking overcoat on a chair near the stove. The

90

logs inside were glowing red, licked by yellow flames.

'I have a little brandy in the kitchen.' She hurried out and returned with a half tumblerful. 'Now, quickly, this is against all the rules – why have you come?'

He sipped the brandy gratefully. 'Thanks, I got very cold out there. I've come because you're in danger, terrible danger. They're on to Fuchs. He's been suspect for months, but now they've decyphered some Russian signals that incriminate him.'

'Can't he get out?'

'No, it's too late. He's watched all the time and they'll arrest him in a few days, maybe even tomorrow. He's bound to name you when they interrogate him. Of course, he'll hold out at first, but they'll threaten him with hanging if he doesn't tell them everything.'

Sonia sat down unsteadily. 'I suppose it was bound to happen sooner or later. You mean they'd arrest me?'

'Of course they'll bloody arrest you. The whole thing is blown wide open – they'll get everybody, the Americans too. You'll be in the dock with Fuchs in a week's time if you don't get out.'

'But I can't leave without orders from Centre.'

'Don't be absurd. Centre may not even know yet. You must go, *at once*, or at least first thing tomorrow morning.' He was less of a grey man when he became animated: for the first time she began to like him. 'Don't forget that you and Fuchs are both British subjects – they'll try you for treason. That could mean a death sentence for you too. Do you *understand*?'

She rearranged his coat, steaming in front of the stove, so that it would dry more quickly. 'Yes, I understand. Thank you for coming – you must be taking a great risk.'

'I'll be okay so long as I can find the car again and don't get pneumonia. Do you have money and visas?'

Sonia sighed – it was providential. She had asked permission for a visit to Berlin over a year before, not having seen her native city since before the war. When there was no response, she had got in touch with her brother Jürgen, who had returned to Berlin with his wife in 1945, asking him to intervene. Still no date had been agreed, but a week ago she had cycled out to the drop on the Banbury road and found the necessary visas for her and the children under the tree root. 'Yes, I have visas for Berlin, all sectors. I don't know how much money I'll need – and what about my husband and son? Len has a broken leg and Michael is at university in Scotland.'

'They'll be okay. There's nothing specific against them, but they should leave as soon as possible.' He pulled an envelope from his suit pocket. 'I've brought some money – I thought you might need it. It's enough for the plane tickets.'

She kissed him lightly on the cheek. He was risking everything by driving out from London like this, when he might well be under suspicion himself; he was a braver man than she had thought. 'Thank you, Alec, thank you for all this. I hope it isn't necessary to save you too one day – but, if it is, I owe you a life. I shan't forget, I promise I shan't forget.'

Next morning she woke the children early, having packed four canvas bags the night before. 'We're going on a holiday,' she explained. 'It's a surprise.'

'But what about school?' exclaimed Nina, now a slim, pretty fourteen-year-old.

Peter yawned. 'I don't want to go unless I can take my toys.'

'There'll be plenty of toys where we're going.'

Len was shocked by the news. Plainly he could not travel until his leg was out of plaster, but did he want to travel at all? The thought of going to the East and never coming back frightened him. Sonia sensed his inner confusion and spoke unemotionally. 'You don't have to come, unless you truly want to.' She stood by the double bed with a cup of tea. 'When you've decided, write to me at my brother's address in Berlin. I'll write to you when I have somewhere to live.'

'But must you go *now*, this morning – with *both* the children?'

'Yes, I must.' She bent down and kissed him. 'Peter is my son too, and he is only six. He needs his mother.'

They walked to the railway halt a mile away and she bought tickets to London. As she waited on the platform

Sonia felt exhausted, for she had been up all night packing and burning her code pads and other papers. Black thoughts crowded into her mind. Both of her parents lay in the churchyard here and she would never see their grave again, nor the cottage that had been the only real home ever shared by her and Len and all the children. In her heart she knew that the parting from Len might be permanent; and would Micha be safe, would they stop him from following her? If she had been alone, not standing on the cold station platform with the trusting children, she would have wept. Then Peter jumped up and down as the train steamed in and Nina, laughing, seized him and opened a carriage door while her mother struggled with the bags.

Following Alec's advice, she left the train at Ealing Broadway and took the Underground to Hounslow West, then a red bus to the row of huts on Hounslow Heath, where the airport at Heathrow was still under construction. She bought tickets for a British European Airways flight to West Berlin, which was leaving in two hours' time. The clerk looked at her curiously when she paid in cash. She had bought a newspaper at Ealing but there was no news of Fuchs in it. Even so, she strolled up and down nervously in the stuffy hut where they waited. She would not feel safe until the plane was in the air and over Germany.

They took off around three o'clock in an old DC-3, the children excited for they had never flown before. The stewardess found them three seats together and offered Sonia a drink as they banked over the grey water of a reservoir south of the airport, before turning due east over London.

'Thank you – do you have any white wine?'

'Certainly, madam. Dry – French, or medium – German?'

'The German wine, please, and orange juice for the children.'

The plane refuelled in Hamburg and reached its destination at seven that evening. The streets near Tempelhof airfield were dark and silent, with nothing to remind her of the glittering city of her youth. They were still in West Berlin and Sonia took the S-Bahn to Friedrichstrasse station, just

93

inside the Russian sector. NKVD guards in green uniforms examined their papers as they left the platform and she found a call-box to telephone her brother's house near the Schlachter See. His wife Marguerite answered. It was a bad line, but through the crackle Sonia explained where they were and heard a half-reassuring 'Jürgen is not here, but I'll come at once.'

It was ten at night before Marguerite arrived. The children were bad-tempered and freezing, huddled on their canvas bags in the draughty station, stared at curiously by passers-by with hungry faces. Marguerite kissed them all, but explained that she had nowhere to take them to sleep. 'Things are very difficult here. Jürgen has gone to the East. Our house is in the American sector and he could not stay in case they arrested him because of his links with Fuchs. It would not be safe for you either; you must not leave the Soviet zone. The city is still in ruins, but we will find you somewhere to sleep.' They crossed the river and wandered through the dark streets from hotel to hotel, Sonia carrying Peter and Nina stumbling with tiredness. Everywhere was full and about midnight the porter of the Hotel Sofia told them of an old couple who let rooms in a street near the Rosenthaler Platz. After another dreary walk Sonia found the place and rang the bell. The landlady took them in and was happy to accept English money for a cold, dirty room on the fourth floor. The children slept in one damp bed and Sonia in the other.

In the morning they went out so that Sonia could find a public telephone and again try to contact her brother. Both Nina and her mother were horrified by their first sight of Berlin in daylight: the district they were in was like a desert. Jagged ruins of bombed houses lined the streets. There were long queues of women at foodstalls and their pinched faces, wrapped in head scarves against an icy wind, stared at Sonia's English clothes with envy and suspicion. Men dressed in rags lay drunk in the gutter. To escape the cold she took the children into a café, but it was as freezing inside as out.

'Have you no heating?' she demanded of the man behind

the bar, awkward at speaking in her own language again after so long.

He looked at her smooth hands with contempt. 'Where have you come from, comrade? Don't you know we can burn coal only every third day – and not much of it even then?'

'No, I am new here. May I have a coffee and hot milk for the children?'

'There is no coffee and no milk. There is soup. Cabbage soup.'

'Is that all?'

'Of course. No meat, no potatoes, just soup.'

'May I have three bowls?'

He held out his hand and she looked at him questioningly. 'How much is it?'

'Give me your identity and ration cards.'

'I'm sorry, I don't have a ration card, yet.'

He withdrew his hand abruptly. 'What are you, with your new shoes and plump children, some sort of capitalist spy? Get out of my café before I report you to the NKVD.'

She was back on the cobbled street lined with piles of rubble, with the children trailing after her. Nina stared at her mother, the full brown eyes in the innocent face suddenly full of horror. 'Mummy, you said it was a holiday. Why have we come to this *awful* place?'

'You said they would have toys,' muttered Peter accusingly. 'I want to go home.' He began to cry.

18

East Berlin

Sarah drove through the drab suburbs of Berlin early in the afternoon. Ugly apartment blocks, hurriedly run up in grey concrete during the fifties, were interspersed with factories and well-equipped children's playgrounds. Compared with any West European capital the people were poorly dressed and there were few cars on the streets, mostly small Polish Fiats, Skodas and Ladas.

She stopped at a phone box in a row by a windy shopping precinct and dialled 220 2431. A man's voice answered, 'British Embassy.'

'May I speak to Miss Richardson?'

'Certainly, madam.' There was a ringing tone and a woman's voice of indeterminate age answered. 'Richardson.'

'My name is Diana Hughes, I was told you might be able to help me.' There was a shuffling of papers in the SIS office and a slight hum on the line, as if a trace had been switched on to check for tapping.

'Yes, I remember. How is your father these days?'

'Well, except for his deafness.' God, thought Sarah, they might dream up some less banal recognition phrases.

'Is he still living in Bournemouth?'

'No, he moved to Weymouth last year.'

'I had forgotten. The man you wanted will meet you in a café on Unter den Linden at three o'clock, the Café Luxembourg. He will be sitting at a table outside unless it is raining. The café is not far from this Embassy should you wish to contact me later.'

'Thank you.' Sarah returned to the car thoughtfully. Nairn had told her to talk to a long-standing agent code-named

Magda: she did not know his real name, but that he was a middle-ranking officer in MfS, the Ministry for State Security. Nairn had shown her a photograph of a large fat man, with receding brown hair and a bulbous drinker's nose. Presumably he would look at home in a café, but it seemed a rather public place to meet.

An hour later she parked the Golf in a side street near the tree-lined shade of Unter den Linden. The café had tables and umbrellas on a terrace outside and Magda was instantly recognizable, nursing a large tankard of beer. He waved to her like an old friend. 'Ingrid! *Wie geht's?*'

She sat down at the little metal table. '*Sehr gut, danke.* Can we talk in English?'

'*Natürlich.*' He beckoned the white-coated waiter and called for a small beer. 'What can I do for you?'

'Our mutual friend in London said that you would advise me on Sonia's present position.'

Magda was wearing a well-cut suit in a fawn material with a hint of gold thread; he leaned forward, resting one elbow in a puddle of beer and withdrawing it in a gesture of irritation that was almost effeminate. Sarah wondered whether he had been given his code-name because he was homosexual. 'She is probably a little worried. Men from the MfS have visited her to enquire about her son, the one who has just been to America. I think he is under suspicion and it rubs off on her.'

'But is she under any real threat?'

'I shall know better in a day or so, after I have been to a routine meeting with the responsible director. I will send a message in the usual way.'

'Is it time for me to see Sonia and proposition her?'

'No, much too early. Leave me to make sure that she feels some pressure first. She won't frighten easily, but she isn't stupid either.'

'Can you really arrange that?'

'Yes.' Magda emptied his *Stein* and called for another one. 'Where have you come from?'

'Thüringia.'

'Why were you there?'

Sarah weighed his need to know, but decided to risk it. 'I was meeting her son.'

The waiter brought another beer and Magda eyed her narrowly across the rim of the half-litre glass. 'The son? But he is under surveillance! You are in danger – they will know your car. Forget about the old woman, just get out at once. You can be in the West in half an hour.'

'I had a feeling there were watchers. Yes, I'll go through the Wall. I've nothing else to do here anyway. Is it safe to use the car – it will attract attention if I just abandon it.'

'It's hired – there are records?'

'Yes.'

'Better take it with you. When did you leave Thüringia?'

'This morning.'

'Were you followed then?'

'For a little way, I suppose by the local Vopos.'

Magda lit a cigarette and considered. 'Those bumpkins will almost certainly report in writing and that will lose a day. I know it sounds bureaucratic and inefficient, but we *are* bureaucratic and inefficient. If you abandon the car, that will increase suspicion of the son. Don't go that way,' he gestured towards the unmistakable outline of the Brandenburg Gate at the end of the boulevard. 'Use one of the southern checkpoints.'

'What happens if I'm stopped?'

'You have genuine visas?'

'Yes, and an Austrian passport.'

'Look innocent and hope for the best.' He gave a deep belly laugh and heads turned at other tables. 'If the worst happens, our jails are no worse than yours, which is not saying a lot.'

'Thanks very much.'

He finished his beer and stood up, leaving some coins on the table. 'There are not many pavement cafés in the Russian sector, you know. Take my arm and look natural, I have just picked you up.'

Sarah did so and they strolled a little way under the lime trees. 'I shall now kiss you and send you on your way with a traditional slap on the bottom,' he chuckled. 'Look like a good German *Mädchen* and enjoy it. Good luck, my dear.

I hope you'll be safe.' His arms round her were reassuring, but she began to feel apprehensive as soon as she turned the corner. The new green Volkswagen with its Austrian number-plates stood out alarmingly in the uniform row of rusty and weather-stained Fiats and Skodas parked by the kerb.

19

Stockholm – 1962

The grey-haired woman with sparkling eyes arranged herself comfortably on a wooden bench. The waters of the lagoon lapped a few feet away, glittering blue in the sun, and a flotilla of ducks converged on the crusts she tossed out to them. Half an hour before she had turned her back on the clustered alleys and spires of Gamla Stan, the old town, and set off down a causeway, past a hundred or more fishing boats and small yachts, tied up with halyards clattering against their metal masts in the breeze. She walked on, past the white schooner that served as a youth hostel, through the trees to the far side of the island. It was September, the beginning of the Swedish autumn, so it was chilly despite the sun; a month ago the shore of Skeppsholmen would have been crowded with sunbathers, but now it was empty.

He arrived twenty minutes later, a stooping figure in a black City overcoat. 'May I join you?' He raised an old felt hat and spoke politely in English.

She smiled up at him: he had grown even greyer in twelve years, but his eyes were the same. 'Of course.' He sat beside her and she started to feed the ducks again. 'Are you safe, not followed?'

'No one knows I am in Sweden. I'm flying back to London from Hong Kong, so I left the plane in Delhi and made my own bookings to get here. I'll be in England as expected tonight. We are quite safe.'

'Good.' She searched his face quizzically, 'Well – you have become very important, I hear. A top man in MI5. Congratulations!'

'It took some doing, believe me, to make the top despite some serious . . . errors of judgement along the way.' He gave a wry smile. 'And you have become a grandmother?'

'Yes, I have several grandchildren.'

'Are you happy to be back in Berlin?'

'It was a little hard at first – the devastation after the war was appalling – but now it is fine.'

'And are the children glad to be in their own country?'

She threw back her head and laughed. 'Sometimes I'm not sure that it really *is* their country, but they cope.'

She studied a white ferry boat chugging towards the flat buildings of the south shore, then turned to him briskly. 'I am here for the Centre. You asked for a meeting and, because you are so valuable they agreed. This is highly exceptional – you must still have a controller in London?'

'Of course, but I wanted to see you again and . . . and you owe me a life.'

'Not quite a life. Fuchs only got fourteen years. He was in jail for nine, as the prison librarian.' She gave a half-smile. 'It could have been worse. Now he's director of the nuclear research centre at Dresden and married to Greta, his child-hood sweetheart.'

'He was damned lucky. If they'd charged him with high treason he'd have hanged. They reduced the charge because the Soviet Union was an ally when he was spying – and I suppose because he was co-operative. You still owe me a life.'

'Yes, of course, and if you need help the Centre will do everything it can for you. You have served them well for twenty years.'

'I hope so.'

'So what has gone wrong? Are you under suspicion? After all this time? Surely not?'

'Not exactly, but I *am* concerned. I have a rather compli-cated message to send and I thought you would ensure that it reached the right destination.'

She looked puzzled, then gave the huge, warm smile he remembered from the Oxford days. 'Tell me, Alec.'

'There *is* suspicion in London. So far as I know, it is not yet directed at me, but there are murmurs that there must be a traitor in MI5 and they are getting too close for comfort.'

'Why is there suspicion?'

101

'Good Lord – how could there *not* be? So many things have gone wrong since the war. Burgess and Maclean started it . . .'

'But that's ancient history now, almost comic!'

'It was not comic at the time, it shook the whole country, it shook every government in the West; and then there were all the other disasters – Cairncross, Pribyl, Vassall, the Molody case. A whole series of defectors going to the Americans, all claiming they couldn't risk London because there was a Soviet agent high in my service.'

'Has this caused you any *serious* problems?'

'Not yet, but there are two cases coming up which may. The danger is always round the corner. That's why I'm here.'

She said nothing, waiting expectantly. He glanced around, but they were still quite alone. 'One concerns a man who was in our intelligence service . . .'

'Philby?'

'Yes, Philby. They are closing in on him. That could lead them to me as well. The other concerns an agent we have in GRU headquarters . . .'

'You mean Colonel Penkovsky?'

'You are very well informed. I have no direct involvement in his case – he is run by SIS of course – but I imagine that he is likely to be arrested soon. This will be a great shock in London and they will want to know who betrayed him. He is the best high level source they have ever had – his exposure will be a monumental disaster.'

Her eyes hardened. 'They briefed me on this when they agreed I could meet you – he has betrayed some of the most critical secrets. Nuclear weapon strategy, the weakness of the Soviet position . . . he has to be stopped.'

'What will happen to him?'

She shrugged. 'I suppose he will be interrogated and put on trial.'

'The GRU can be harsh on renegades in its own ranks. Will he be tortured?'

She glanced at him curiously. 'I've no idea. I suppose it depends how co-operative he is. What else would you expect for someone in a position of trust who has betrayed so much?'

102

'I don't know . . . that is all alien to me. I had a different vision back in the war.'

'So did many of us, but it is too late to be squeamish now.' She paused but he remained silent, staring at the water, and she studied him thoughtfully. If he was worried about the traitor Penkovsky . . . momentarily she pictured him before a warm fire in a West End club, stretched out in an old-fashioned leather armchair while the agents he had betrayed froze and starved in camps or lay in unmarked graves – foolish Ukrainian nationalists, KGB officers who found God, little bureaucrats who needed the money. Did that trouble him too? Did he waver whenever his liberal conscience was offended? 'There was never time for us to talk in the past, Alec,' she spoke hesitantly. 'But one thing has always puzzled me. You went to Oxford, you are so English . . . Yet you became a Marxist, you *volunteered* to help us, no one forced you. Even for me, that can be hard to understand.'

'Does it matter any more? I have never asked why you joined the KPD when you were seventeen.' He gave a half-smile. 'No one asks the Pope why he is a Christian. It is self-evident, part of life.'

'Is it?'

'The revolution changed my world as well as yours. I felt one had to choose . . .' he shrugged. 'I suppose I chose the side I believed in most – the one with the greater strength in the long run.'

'And has that been enough to live your whole life half in the shadows?'

'It has sometimes been lonely, very lonely.'

She smiled at the typically British understatement. 'And the people walking past on the pavement outside your office in Mayfair; they would say you are betraying them. Does that trouble you?'

'There is no need for these questions, Sonia. I've been fighting with you for twenty years.' He was suddenly fierce. 'It is a war and I do what I must, you know that as well as I do.'

'And in a war there are bound to be casualties,' she said gently.

'I well understand that.'

It was enough; and after twenty years he deserved to be trusted. She became businesslike again. 'So what do you want for yourself now – to get out to the East?'

'If necessary I've always had that option, but no. I can go on – my nerve is better now than in the war – but I must be protected.'

'You would be more use if you stayed, but *how* can you be protected?'

'MI5 has a traitor. If I'm to be safe, we must throw suspicion on somebody else.'

Sonia nodded sagely. 'Somebody else at the top?'

'Exactly.'

Sarah passed safely through the southern checkpoint at Sonnenallee. The road ran back into West Berlin through a small forest and half an hour later she dumped her hired car at Tegel. She caught BA 775 to London at six-thirty in the evening and landed at Heathrow shortly after eight-twenty. A quick phone call found Nairn at the flat in Chiswick and he arranged to meet her an hour later, at a safe house in Richmond.

20

London

'Will it work?' Sir James Simon studied the tips of his fingers thoughtfully.

'God knows, but it's all there is.'

They were sitting side by side at the long table in Simon's room at the Cabinet Office, dusty files from the forties spread out before them. Simon's eyes were beginning to smart from the blue smoke curling from Nairn's well-chewed pipe. He gestured at the faded pages of typescript. 'There's no evidence here that she was a double agent, but I *am* mystified by these two years between the end of 'forty-seven and her flight in 'fifty. She carried on for more than two years after she'd virtually admitted being an agent to MI5 and the police. Is that *possible*? Whoever Alec was, could he have protected her so well?'

'I think he did, but there must have been suspicions in Moscow; they're suspicious people by nature. There she was, an agent working alone out in Oxfordshire, with much more freedom than usual, presumably because Fuchs was such an important source and she had his confidence. Then he was arrested, but she escaped. He got fourteen years, narrowly escaped death, while she was safe in East Berlin before he was even tried . . . I can't believe that someone over there didn't suspect she'd been turned and betrayed Fuchs to save her own skin.'

'Do *you* believe that?'

'No, I don't. I'm sure she was a brave woman and a deeply committed Marxist, one of the best agents of all time – but she hasn't been allowed to do much since 1950 and she hasn't been treated particularly well. She's been suspect – and vulnerable.'

'Vulnerable enough to defect? Even now when she's nearly eighty?'

'She's had a rough time, you know. There's still resentment of her origins – wealthy, Jewish, intellectual. Antisemitism's particularly strong in East Germany. She gave them her whole life, but now she lives in obscurity, struggles on some kind of small pension. There are enemies who'd like to make her life even harder: she's unwanted, a hang-over from a different generation. If her son and his girlfriend defect, and we drop a few broad hints that she double-crossed them back in 1947, she'll be in dead trouble.'

'Is the threat enough to get her out?'

'Possibly. I'm not certain yet.'

'Can we build up pressure on her, to make sure?'

'That's what I hoped to do, but Magda says the son is already under suspicion, so maybe Sonia is too. If we don't move at once, it may be too late to get her out, even if she's willing to come.'

'It's dangerous.'

'It's *bloody* dangerous – but soon it may also be impossible.'

'And even if we do give her asylum, why should she help us?'

'She'll damn well have to, won't she? Or we'll send her back and they'll stick her in a labour camp to die.'

Simon winced. 'Sometimes I feel that you have an unpleasantly ruthless streak, David.'

Nairn rounded on him. 'Not me, Jim. I was against this whole thing from the start, but *you* insisted. *You're* the one who's so desperate to prove the case against Carteret.'

'Aren't *you*?'

'I'm mildly curious, but I wouldn't have chosen to burn Sonia to find out. You chose that, so don't get all mealy-mouthed when you see what's entailed. Sarah's taken some nasty risks over there to get us this far; if it goes wrong, Sonia could end up dead. As could Sarah if we send her back.'

Simon forced a smile. 'I do understand all that, David.'

106

The Viennese charm started to flow like whipped cream on *Sachertorte*. 'But I see no alternative. Box 500 must be made clean and if that means risks, so be it.'

The next day Nairn held a council of war at Edge Manor, once again including Colonel Thorne of SAS for part of the time. Sarah took notes all day, trying to look efficient with fair hair up and wearing a tweed suit. The most difficult part was handing the finished product to Pam to be typed up that evening. She had brought Pam down from the Cut for no other purpose, because she was not only officially secure – PV'd daughter of a long-trusted Regimental Sergeant Major in the Guards – but discreet even with close colleagues. Now she sat there at five o'clock, plumply pretty with dark curls, looking daggers: for a man she would do anything, but she hated taking orders from a girl of her own age.

'Three numbered copies, please, Pam,' Sarah said firmly. 'Sir David wants to read through it at eight o'clock.'

'I wanted to go out for the evening. It's not a bleedin' war is it?'

'No, Pam, but it *is* urgent, so I'd be grateful if you'd get on with it.'

'Couldn't it wait till morning?'

'No, Pam.' Sarah thought how much she would like to kick the girl's fat arse. 'And you knew perfectly well what was involved when you agreed to come down with me – so just *do* it. Okay?'

Nairn appeared as Pam stalked out. 'Let's go for a drink,' he said. There was a snort from the girl vanishing through the door, but he ignored it. 'I thought the Cobb Arms at Lyme.'

He drove himself in the official blue Rover and in half an hour they were descending the hill into Lyme Regis. Evening sun made the sea blue, lapping the hazy coast which curved down to Portland Bill, and the town clustered round its church tower. Nairn parked by the Cobb where the tide was in, fishing boats bobbing between the two stone breakwaters that enclosed the harbour.

He took Sarah's arm and they walked along the quay, in the lee of the wall that sheltered them from a cold westerly

107

breeze. She matched his stride and thought how much younger he looked than when they had first met. In the last six months he'd recaptured all the vigour of a man in . . . well, she smiled to herself, in his *forties*. 'We can't very well talk about work in the pub, David.'

'No.'

'Before we get there I've been wondering – what actually *happened* back in 1963? I mean, after all this suspicion, how did the real investigation start?'

21

Lyme Regis

'It was Embling who started it. He was an assistant director
in D Branch, counter-espionage, and analysing the situation
early in 1963, just after Philby had scarpered. Penkovsky
had been arrested the previous October and was in jail in
Moscow; they knew he'd reveal everything under torture
before they put him on trial. He was sentenced to death that
May, of course, though he seems to have been kept alive in
a camp for endless interrogation and probably committed
suicide. But who had betrayed him?

'Embling listed everything that had gone wrong in the
eighteen years since the war and concluded that the service
was leaking like a sieve. He also thought it had gone from
bad to worse in the last seven years, while Carteret had been
Director-General and Fell his deputy. Nobody but one of
those two could have had the access to cause so much
mayhem. Only a year before he had been sent to Washington
to hear the debriefing of a major Russian defector, Golitsyn,
at Ashford Farm. The man had been insistent that MI5 had
a traitor at the top. Embling didn't know where to turn.
Eventually he made an appointment to see Stephen Black,
who had run Five before becoming chief of our outfit.

'Black thought about it for a day, then rang Embling and
advised him to go to Carteret and accuse Fell.'

'Why? Surely Carteret was the prime suspect?'

'Oh yes, but what else could they do? They both knew
that this meant Fell would be investigated first, even though
they believed him to be innocent; but they reasoned that
once an enquiry had started, it would get a momentum of
its own. Carteret would be nailed in the end, despite his
seemingly invulnerable position.

'Embling walked in on Carteret about six that evening and spelt out his conclusions, slanting them towards Fell. He thought it odd that Carteret hardly reacted; he didn't seem surprised, or shocked – and certainly didn't try to defend his deputy. He seemed almost pleased and took Embling out to dinner at the Travellers' Club. Embling thought this was to carry on the discussion. In fact they just made small-talk, but Carteret called a secret meeting at his house in Campden Hill Square a few days later and the hunt was on. It was kept secret from most of the office, of course, and just five or six people were indoctrinated.

'Fell had been getting on badly with Carteret for some time and shortly afterwards announced that he wanted to retire that September, which gave them only five months to study him in action and prove a case, if there was one. He had a traditional background: Winchester and Oxford. Seemed to have had left-wing sympathies when young, but then became staunchly conservative – the sort of surface change you might expect in a penetration agent. Joined Five in 1939, when he was thirty-four, worked on right-wing extremists and subversion during the war, then on counter-espionage until he became deputy DG in 1956. He lived near Chobham Common with his wife and two kids and belonged to a classy yacht club on the Isle of Wight. Either he was dead straight or he'd erected a beautiful right-wing middle-class façade.'

'What did he do before 'thirty-nine?' asked Sarah.

'He was a journalist and then in the Conservative Party research department.'

'What was there against him?'

'Everything and nothing. It was all circumstantial. He'd defended Philby, messed up the Pontecorvo case so that the man got away to Moscow in 1950, cast doubt on the credibility of defectors like Golitsyn. For a clever man, he'd made a lot of mistakes that had done serious damage. They recruited some amateur watchers from our service and trailed him to and from Waterloo Station every day. They watched his home too. He sometimes went out by car as soon as he got home, to lonely spots on the common – possibly dead letter boxes? So they passed identifiable and

110

doctored intelligence reports across his desk, to see if they would show up in intercepts of radio traffic from the Russian Embassy.'

'Did it work?'

'No. They even rigged up a hidden TV camera in his office and watched him. He did nothing suspicious, but always looked utterly miserable; sometimes he just stared into space and sat with his head in his hands. Once he looked desperately at the communicating door into Carteret's room and groaned *Why are you doing this to me?*'

'What happened in the end?'

'Nothing. Some of them thought he might be guilty. It *was* all circumstantial evidence, but in a way it seemed to add up. He was curiously isolated, despite being deputy DG; nobody really knew him, quite a few disliked him or felt suspicious. But there was nothing really hard and he wasn't interrogated. He wasn't supposed to know he was under suspicion – but I think he did.'

'You mean he just retired?'

'In September 1963. Carteret flew straight off to Washington to warn the CIA and FBI that they might have been compromised, which was odd – unless he had something to hide himself – because nothing had actually been *proved* against Fell, nothing at all.'

They had reached the end of the Cobb and were sitting on a low stone wall, sheltered from the wind by a fishing shed and looking out over grey sea to Portland. 'Did it leak out in the office?'

'Good Lord, yes. Leconfield House was stiff with rumours and the top brass were all told officially. Morale was rock-bottom. Fell hadn't been a popular figure, but he *had* been deputy head of the whole outfit. Yet he'd been interrogated as a suspected traitor. He kept his pension and the CB, but many thought he'd been a scapegoat, that it had to be Carteret – and *he* was still the boss. All trust had gone. As far as the Americans were concerned, not to mention the Australians, Canadians, New Zealanders and our own government, MI5 was the pits.'

They both studied the white-flecked waves. 'Clever old Russians,' said Sarah finally.

22

Devon

The plan was completed late the following morning. Nairn and Sarah were alone in the conference room at Edge, blue typewritten sheets spread out on the table. In two days' time Sarah would meet Magda again, in West Berlin, and brief him on every aspect of the threat to Sonia. Nairn thought it too risky for Sarah to enter the East again, so Magda would be the messenger. He would arrive at Sonia's apartment unannounced and spell out the dangers that faced her.

'She's brave enough,' said Nairn. 'But not stupid. She'll realize how vulnerable she is now.'

Magda would offer a way out: come to the West and we'll treat you with respect. After a short debriefing, you and your husband can live in comfort and safety for the rest of your days. You're in danger, but we'll take care of you. Sarah nodded. 'But *how* do we get her out, David?'

'In a good old-fashioned way. We can't risk the Berlin crossing points, or any of the East German land borders; she might be recognized and stopped, particularly if she's already under suspicion. But it's still possible to lift people out from the Baltic coast. It's only a hundred-mile drive from Berlin, through empty country – you can do it in less than three hours at night.'

'Aren't there dozens of coastguard stations and patrol boats?'

'Of course, but it's a longish coastline with plenty of remote spots. It's not too hard to run in a submarine, underwater so their radar misses it, then pick a couple of people off a beach with an inflatable. They once thought of rescuing Penkovsky that way, you know. It's quick and usually works if they can just get to the coast without being

112

followed – if Magda can scare them into going the same night in Sonia's own car, we'd have her here within twenty-four hours.'

'But is Magda that persuasive, David? Despite the threat, will she really up sticks and leave just like that, at *her* age?'

'I honestly don't know, but it's the only chance we have.' He put the papers into a safe, closed the steel door and spun the two combination dials until they clicked shut. 'Let's go for a stroll down by the lake and I'll tell you the end of the Fell story.'

'After Fell retired, the unrest about penetration continued. Carteret was pushed into doing more so he set up a joint MI5/MI6 committee to go on with the enquiry – if you don't know what to do, set up a committee. The next code-word on the list was Sanctuary so it was called the Sanctuary Committee. Carteret didn't provide it with much in the way of resources and called it the "Gestapo", but he didn't obstruct it directly.

'Embling was on the committee and produced a list of forty events which he thought showed that Five was penetrated and that Carteret or Fell was a Soviet agent. It was all pretty weird, since the committee was reporting its conclusions to Carteret – but also to Stephen Black of our service, so Carteret was no longer a free agent. They wanted to interrogate Fell, but Carteret refused to allow it. There was some feeling that interrogation would clear Fell, so that only increased suspicion against Carteret.

'In 1965 Carteret retired and, after a couple of years more – incredibly there seems to have been no sense of urgency – Fell was finally asked to return to the office. He was taken to a safe house in South Audley Street and confronted by Alan Knight, a retired Royal Marines colonel, who was a highly skilled interrogator.'

'How do you know, David? Were you on the committee?'

'Yes, there were three of us from SIS.'

'What happened?'

'Knight ran through all the evidence against Fell and everything was taped – I've listened to it all a dozen times. Fell co-operated in going over virtually his whole life. When

113

it came to specific accusations, he admitted nothing. There was an answer to everything. Yes, he took evasive action when he was tailed to Waterloo; how should he know that the watchers were British and not from a hostile service? He agreed that it would be disastrous if all the Soviet and other target embassies knew exactly who was being watched and when, but he knew nothing of an unused drawer in the conference table in the room where he held a meeting every week to settle the targets for Five's own watchers, nor of their suspicions that it had held a concealed tape-recorder. Yes, he had drawn a map of Chobham Common they'd found in his wastepaper basket. No, it wasn't for a rendezvous with the KGB, it was to plan a charity paper-chase that one of his grandchildren was taking part in. And then on and on through every case that had gone wrong while he was head of D Branch, responsible for counter-espionage, and then deputy to Carteret. That was the real stuff, of course, but he just claimed that everything was down to chance or bad luck. He never cracked.'

'Was there a conclusion?'

'Not really. Some thought him guilty, some innocent. He went back into the obscurity of retirement, the same tall, stooping man that nobody knew. He was even offered immunity from prosecution, but he still denied everything, and now he's been visited every month for nearly twenty years, just in case he changes his mind.'

'It's horrific, David. Do *you* think he was guilty?'

'I simply don't know – that's one reason why Sonia is so important. If the poor bastard was innocent, he was treated shamefully.'

'Was he interrogated again?'

'No. The only way for Sanctuary to go after that was to interrogate Carteret, which was almost unthinkable. The retired head of MI5 himself, who had left honourably with a knighthood, the top man in security for nine years. It would be a hell of a step to take.'

'But they took it?'

'Yes. Three years later, in 1970.'

114

23

Oxford

Nairn did not return straight to London. Months before, on a quiet Thursday, he had accepted an invitation to Oxford that evening, for dinner at a college where the Senior Tutor had long been a talent spotter for the service. Usually he enjoyed an evening of good food and witty, if sometimes affected, conversation, but today it was a damned nuisance. Sonia weighed too heavily on his mind, a thousand other things were piling up at Century House and he would have preferred to drive back to London with Sarah, stopping at one of the country pubs along the way.

As it was, Sarah caught the train from Taunton and Nairn drove up the M5 to Bristol, then east along the M4 to Swindon, where he followed side roads to Oxford. By six-thirty he was parked in the college and a porter had shown him to the Fellows' guest room, which looked out into a quadrangle surrounded by a medieval cloister. When he opened the window young voices rang up from below. He peered through the branches of wistaria to see a group of students rehearsing a play on the billiard table lawn; his own university days at Glasgow had been nothing like this.

Before dinner his host took him for sherry in the Fellows' smoking room, after which the twenty or so who were dining put on black gowns and shuffled into the hall. The high table was on a dais at one end, under high Gothic windows. Nairn was placed at the right of the Master, rather wishing that he were in the body of the hall, which was full of young men and women who looked considerably more interesting. At the nearest table was a pretty girl with long fair hair who reminded him of Sarah.

The meal was served rapidly and within forty-five minutes

they all rose abruptly, someone muttered a Latin grace and the high table processed out. They did not return to the smoking room, but walked in a ragged line round the cloister to a common room where another long table had been set for dessert. Here they sat down for a second meal of fruit, nuts and cheese. Claret had been served with dinner; now port and marsala circled the table.

Nairn had covered most of his business with the Senior Tutor before dinner, so he relaxed and chatted amiably to those around him. 'I can never recall where you work in Whitehall, Sir David,' queried an elderly don with a decidedly Hungarian accent.

'The Foreign Office,' smiled Nairn, sipping his port. The whole performance always astounded him – he could survive for a week on one dinner from the college. No doubt the place was touched by the recession like everything else, but there was no sign of it in the confidence that flowed from five hundred years of history and a thirty-million-pound endowment. For twenty years Nairn had deliberately increased the number of recruits from working-class and non-Oxbridge backgrounds; but there was still a hell of a lot of brain power in this town and his visits were usually productive. So were his visits to Leeds, but the dinners weren't so good.

After a while Nairn's host excused them and they strolled by the river. The don ran through the young men and women he had earmarked and Nairn agreed that he should encourage them to put in for the Diplomatic Service. They would then be approached if they survived the selection tests.

'It's nice of you to find time to come down to see us, David. Are you busy at the moment?'

The aroma of Nairn's pipe smoke floated through the dark. 'The usual grind,' he grunted. 'Nothing worth talking about.'

Next morning he was woken by a phone call from the porters' lodge soon after seven. 'There's a bloke here for you, Sir David. On a motorbike. Says he's from your office.'

'What does he look like?'

'Dead scruffy.'

'Yes – that sounds like one of mine – send him round.'

Nairn pulled on his dressing gown and met the despatch rider at the top of the narrow staircase from the cloisters. The man waited in the sitting room while Nairn retreated into his bedroom to open the pouch; the brown leather was stained with use, stamped with a black EIIR above the heavy brass lock. It contained a deciphered telegram from Berlin. Last night, he read, Sonia had left her flat in a military looking car and been followed to a government office in a forest outside the city. So far she had not returned and they thought she had probably gone on unobserved to another destination. Damn. All bets were off until she reappeared. *If* she reappeared.

After a leisurely breakfast he threw his bag into the back of the car and nosed out into the stream of bicycles in the Oxford side-street. It was a sunny day and, with the Sonia operation interrupted, he felt disinclined to drive straight back to London. A sudden impulse made him turn north, instead of south for the motorway, and he left town by the Woodstock Road. He was soon passing the gates of Blenheim Palace and, in about half an hour, the small stone town of Chipping Norton. The turning for Great Rollright was two miles further, on the right.

It was a tiny village, isolated in a fold of the hills, curiously remote despite being so close to Oxford. On his first visit, fifteen years ago, he had seen at once why Sonia had chosen it. The Firs was close to the centre of the village, stone built with a slate roof and peeling paintwork. He parked in the lane and walked into the yard behind the house, his feet crunching on freshly laid gravel. The kitchen door was open and he knocked gently on its frame.

The woman was new to him. She had an open, gentle face and was surrounded by eight children, some of whose faces had a pinched look that had known fear or hunger. 'Hello,' she smiled. 'You from the council?'

'No, not from the council.'

'Oh, I thought you might have come about the damage done by that teenage arsonist they sent – he almost burnt the house down, you know.' She spoke brightly, with no trace of anger, and before long Nairn was inside, accepting a cup of tea and sitting down at the kitchen table. 'You must be a foster mother?'

'Yes – how clever of you to guess!' She had a smile that radiated something close to pure goodness. Two of the children were starting to pull on shoes and outdoor coats. 'The school bus will be here soon.'

Nairn glanced round the kitchen. It had not changed much in fifteen years, probably not since Sonia's time. There was a flagstone floor and low ceiling, a black iron range in the fireplace. The woodwork was painted a dull institutional red, which had a wartime look about it. 'Have you been here long?'

'About six years.'

He nodded. 'I came here once before, but that was fifteen years back.'

Finally she showed a glimmer of curiosity. 'Did you want something?'

'Nothing particular, but I'm interested in a family who lived here during the war.'

'You must mean the Beurtons?' She spoke casually while brushing hair with one hand and trying to spread jam with the other, but he sensed that he was not her first unexpected visitor. 'Wasn't she a spy or something?'

'Probably.'

'That was long before I bought the place, of course, but she sounds rather nice to me.'

'Does she? How do you know?'

'Oh, I've had all her children here at different times. They came from Berlin.'

'Really?' Nairn could not help sounding astonished. 'Are you in touch with her, then?'

'Good Lord no, my dear. Her youngest son just turned up on the doorstep about five years ago. No warning or anything. He said he'd left here when he was six and it was his first visit back from East Germany. He'd been allowed to come to some sort of scientific meeting in London, so he'd decided to come and see his old home. He was in tears on the doorstep, it meant so much to him.'

'What name did he use? How old was he?'

118

'He was in his thirties and used the name Peter Werner.'

'Did he stay?'

'No, but the daughter did. She came about a year later, also without warning, and stayed a week. She slept in her old bedroom. An absolutely lovely person, said she was nearly fifty and had a grandchild, but didn't look anything like that age.'

Nairn made no further effort to explain why he had come, but he was sure she was being totally frank with him, holding nothing back. She had no guile. Her life centred around the foster children, who plainly consumed every minute of every exhausting day. 'Was it also the daughter's first visit to England since leaving after the war?'

'Oh yes, I'm sure it was. I think it had been very difficult for her to get permission to come, particularly as it was just for a kind of holiday.'

'Did she come alone?'

'I suppose so, she was by herself when she came here. She just stayed with us – I didn't ask her a lot of questions.'

'And the other son?'

'He was here perhaps a year ago. I barely saw him. He was in a car outside when I came home one afternoon and we chatted. He said he was on a course at the Shakespeare Institute in Stratford, so perhaps he's an actor.'

'What name did he use?'

'Michael something . . . I can't remember.'

'Friedmann?'

'Yes, Michael Friedmann.' The eyes in the beatific face hardened slightly. 'You're not from the police or anything, are you?'

'No, I'm not from the police. I'm just interested in the family.' Any number of phoney reasons sprang into his mind, but he left them unsaid. He did not want to lie to her.

'They were all very nice, delightful people.' She bustled the remaining children out to play in the yard. 'But they didn't mention their father and mother – in fact I thought they must be dead.'

'Did you ever tell anybody else that they had been here?'

'Anybody else? No, why on earth should I? The younger son came before I knew the rumours in the village about his mother and later I felt it was none of my business. Would you like some more tea?' She emptied the dregs of the huge pot into his cup. 'Oh dear, perhaps I should make some more.'

'Thank you, but there's no need. Tell me, what did the three children look like?'

'Handsome family. The daughter, Nina, was slim and beautiful. Michael was thickset and dark, the other son thinner, but also dark.'

'I have some photographs which I think may be of one of the sons.'

'How interesting – I'd love to see them.'

Nairn pulled an envelope from his inside pocket and began to move the half-finished plates of cornflakes to spread out the prints. 'Would you be able to put a name to them?'

She peered, then stood up. 'I think I may need my spectacles.'

Later that morning a green Vauxhall arrived outside the bungalow near Milton Keynes. Richard Fell eyed it malevolently through the net curtains of his front room; he was tall, with sunken cheeks, and looked older than a man in his mid-seventies. He knew that there was no point ignoring the ring at the door, even though he was alone in the house: they would just return tomorrow, and the day after and the day after that. There was no way of avoiding them.

Fell opened the front door and made no attempt to greet the man outside. He wore the same cavalry tie and dark three-piece suit. 'Good morning, Richard,' he smiled. 'May I come in?'

'If you must, damn you. I've nothing to say – you surely understand that after twenty years of this nonsense.'

'I live in hope, Richard. Let's just run over a few things – maybe something will occur to you if you try really hard?'

'For God's sake, man. They've wrecked my life – do they want to drive me insane as well?'

24

Berlin

The Friedrich Engels Park was in Köpenick, a green area of woods and lakes seven miles south-east of the city centre. It was also not far from Sonia's apartment, but Peter was careful to avoid that neighbourhood. He left his car near the entrance to the park and walked towards the sausage stall. The paths under the trees were empty except for the occasional courting couple, seeking a little privacy away from their overcrowded flats and holding hands in the dusk.

The stall by the lake was shut and he found the crack in the steps without difficulty. Sitting down on the concrete, as if studying the rippling black expanse of water, he felt for the papers. They were a bulky package in a long envelope. He placed them in his inside pocket and hurried back to the car.

Sonia had returned, so Sarah was finally on her way back to Berlin. She had become Ingrid Ruckenbauer again and spent the night under that name in a modern hotel near Heathrow Airport. At eleven o'clock, unable to sleep, she went downstairs to a bar festooned with palm trees and creeper, a swimming pool in its centre, and ordered Campari and soda.

Sarah sat alone at a white plastic table, wondering why she was so dangerously attracted to a man more than twice her age. The truth was that her contemporaries were good for a night or two and she could captivate them with sexual skills that she had, at first, found slightly shocking; but however hard she tried she always somehow felt too grown-up for them. It was partly just that she was nearly six feet tall and they generally seemed to be shorter; but more the process of accelerated experience that came from two years in the service. Her knowledge of the sheer awfulness of people and governments set her apart from other girls of nearly twenty-three, much as she wished it otherwise. Young estate agents at parties thought she was a typist with a head full of cotton wool and good for an easy lay. But David was different and exciting to be with: powerful, worldly-wise and, in her company, vital like a man of no more than forty. He treated her in a way that made her feel she was betraying neither mind nor body by being feminine; he made her feel less of a mess.

She gave a wry smile and sighed. She knew she was being ridiculous, but she had been with him until three hours ago at a safe house in Richmond, going over every last detail before leaving for Berlin. At the end he had talked more about the investigation of Carteret and she wished that she had known him then, twenty years ago, for it had clearly disturbed him in ways that she wanted to understand.

'I asked Black to take me off the bloody committee after Fell retired, but he refused. I even thought of resigning, but what else was I qualified to do to earn a living?' They were upstairs, in a room overlooking Richmond Green, heavy brown curtains shutting out the street where people were parking to go to the theatre.

'Why were you so against it?'

'I thought we were all going crazy. After Fell retired, we went on meeting and examining the evidence. We sat round a table in Curzon Street, trying to prove that Carteret was a spy, while he sat upstairs waiting for our report. He went on as Director-General for another two years, until the end of 1965. It was a lunatic situation.

'Finally Carteret retired to Somerset and Roxburgh Smith took over as DG. That made it easier to run the enquiry – at least the main suspect was off the premises – but my heart wasn't in it. Sometimes I felt he was as innocent as Fell and the whole thing was paranoia. In which case what were we doing persecuting them, ruining the last years of their lives after decades of faithful service? Sometimes I felt sure he was guilty; in which case, just what was this witches' brew of Marxism that had led him to endure a whole lifetime of danger and betrayal? How the devil could we have let him get to the top of the organization on which our ultimate security depended?

'It raised too many questions for which there was no answer. I just wanted to get back to some good old-fashioned spying in Vienna or Rio or Singapore, before this can of worms turned me off the whole business. And we never reached a bloody conclusion. It was clear that there had been a Soviet agent high in MI5 – too many defectors had told the same story for there to be much doubt about that. But could we be *certain* it was Carteret? It was mind bending.'

'What about Sonia?' Sarah asked.

Nairn shook his head. 'No one had heard of Sonia then, so Carteret's Shanghai connection didn't seem as important as it does now. But there was plenty of other stuff against him. He had gone to extraordinary lengths to obstruct investigations into a number of suspected traitors – some of whom had turned out to be guilty. He had pursued Fell, but then prevented an interrogation which might have shown him innocent – so, some thought, keeping him under suspicion and diverting attention from himself. The whole nine years when he'd been in charge had seen a chain of disasters; either he was dead useless – or working brilliantly for an enemy . . . and if he *was* useless how the hell had he become head of the service in the first place?

'Silly little things came up, too. He had a habit of staying late in the office, till about eight o'clock, then walking home across Hyde Park, not using his chauffeured car. Staying late is quite a standard way of copying papers secretly, parks are standard places for drops or clandestine meetings, but maybe he just worked slowly and liked a walk to unwind?'

'Pretty thin evidence of treason.'

'Yes, each bit was thin, but there were an awful lot of bits. Maybe the totality . . .?' Nairn smiled and she wished she could read the message in those kind but penetrating eyes. 'It doesn't seem so distasteful twenty years on and I'd like to know the answer. It's not quite the matter of life and death that Jim Simon thinks – but it's done so much damage that we need an end to it. If Carteret *was* a traitor, I can't

123

believe he didn't make arrangements for a successor . . . that's what matters now, we *must* know, so do your best in Berlin, Sarah, won't you?'

PART FOUR

The Third Betrayal

25

Berlin

Sarah arrived at Tegel on flight BA 780, just before one o'clock, and took a taxi to the hotel she had booked by phone. It was in the Tiergarten district, not far from the Brandenburg Gate, and she registered with her Austrian passport. In this city of spies she would take great care to remain anonymous; there would be no contact with the SIS office at Hitler's Olympic stadium, although they would watch her back and make contact secretly if Nairn sent a change in her instructions. Otherwise she would behave as a tourist, meet Magda when he came over from the East early that evening, brief him and be back in London within twenty-four hours.

The hotel room was small, but equipped with a bathroom, colour television, electric kettle and coffee bags. Sarah unpacked and put on a dark blue skirt and white sweater, for it was autumn and several degrees colder than in London. She descended in the tiny lift and found a café not far away where she settled down with a large coffee and a slice of nut and cherry *Torte* laced with cream. She was eating and drinking too much, but the solitary life of the bogus Ingrid had to be filled up somehow. The cryptic notes she had made at Edge were in her handbag and she began to read through them slowly. Magda would have a difficult task that evening, perhaps an impossible one, and she wanted to give him all the ammunition she could.

Nairn spent the early part of the afternoon at the Navy communications centre in Northwood, poring over charts with a Rear-Admiral in a lounge suit. The coast of East Germany bulged out into the Baltic at Stralsund, where a narrow channel separated the island of Rugen from the mainland. The submarine was lying in shallow water to the east. 'Is it really safe from detection there?' asked Nairn. 'I know their radar won't pick it up, but what about patrol boats?'

'Perfectly safe,' beamed the Rear-Admiral over his gold-rimmed half-moon spectacles. 'There are subs sitting on the bottom off hostile coasts all over the world, including those carrying the nuclear missiles of ourselves and three other countries. If a coastal patrol picks it up on its echo sounder or whatever, they'll probably think it belongs to the Russians. It would take them half a day to check – and by tomorrow morning it should be gone.'

'It could have to wait another twenty-four hours.'

'I'm still not too worried, but I think it might be better if you can get all this tied up tonight.'

Nairn was driven back to London in a Navy Daimler, along the elevated section of the A40 past White City and Paddington. He reached Century House at five o'clock.

Peter's flat was near Karlshorst and the balding German had spent the afternoon watching television and smoking nervously. It should all be over in twenty-four hours and he was already feeling relieved; the last month had been a much greater strain than he had expected. Occasionally he went to the window and glanced out through the net curtains. A different car was always parked in the street and he was sure it was a watcher, presumably from the British Embassy. They would see him drive off in an hour or two, but no matter. He was not waiting for the promised phone call from the damned British. It would be a complication if the watcher followed him, but he did not think that would happen. The *Dummkopf* would wait for Peter to come back, because he wasn't supposed to be leaving yet. He would have to wait a hell of a long time.

At five o'clock he let himself out of the apartment and took the lift to the underground garage where he put his case in the boot of the Mercedes. He gunned the big car up the ramp to the street and turned right past the front of the building. The watcher's car was a small Fiat; it made no attempt to follow him. He accelerated south, past the yachts on Lake Muggel, towards the autobahn that rings the city. He found some classical music on the car radio; a tenor and a bass were singing the duet from Bizet's *Pearl Fishers* and he joined in, suddenly lighthearted that his ordeal was coming to an end.

It was about a mile before the autobahn that he realized he was being followed. A black Volga with four men was maintaining a constant distance behind. When he accelerated, so did they, then slowed as he braked on a corner. Damn those British idiots. He was almost relieved when he saw the roadblock ahead. After all, he was still a citizen of the GDR driving lawfully in his own country while they, with a bit of luck, would be stopped from leaving the city limits.

A steel barrier had been placed across the road and two police cars were parked on the verge. Four Vopos with sub-machine guns stood near them. A fifth had just guided a truck round the end of the barrier and turned to stop the Mercedes with a white baton. The road was bordered by pine trees and he noticed a grey van standing in their shadow.

The Vopo approached as he wound down the car window. 'Your identity card, please.'

The false papers were hidden under the back seat and he produced the card showing his real identity. The Vopo glanced at the name and photograph and waved to the others, who surrounded the car. He saw the black Volga draw up and four more men in plain clothes got out with drawn pistols. Suddenly he began to feel frightened.

'Get out,' snapped the Vopo.

'But why? I have done nothing. I am on urgent official business and you have no right to stop me!'

The door was wrenched open and two Vopos leaned in. His arms were seized and he was dragged out, the metal of the handbrake tearing his trousers and gouging a wound in his leg. He struggled, but they were too strong for him. 'Let me go!' he shouted. 'Can't you see who I am? There will be trouble later, I promise you!' A Vopo kicked him hard in the groin and he doubled up, retching. His right sock was getting soaked in blood.

'We *know* who you are,' spat one of the men in plain clothes. 'And we have orders to arrest you.'

'But this is ridiculous!' He got no further before he was knocked to the ground and felt boots smashing into his body from all directions. He screamed in pain as they seized his legs and dragged him across the tarmac to the grey van, scraping the skin from his hands and one cheek. They threw him into the back of the van. Before they slammed its door, he noticed the Vopo already removing the steel barrier and waving on the queue of traffic. Another was slashing at the back seat of the Mercedes with a knife. They had been waiting for him.

26

London – 1970

They assembled at 41 South Audley Street at nine in the morning: Nairn, Simon, Kirk, Knight. Only Knight would face Carteret across the table, while the others listened upstairs. Every word would be taped – if, of course, Carteret agreed to talk at all.

It had taken them time to convince Roxburgh Smith, the new Director-General, that Carteret should be interrogated. He had resisted, saying that it was grotesque to drag the man, who had recommended his own appointment as successor, from retirement and treat him 'like a criminal'. In the end he had agreed, but insisted on doing it in as civilized a way as possible. The committee had wanted to pick Carteret up at home without warning and subject him to interrogation straightaway. Instead he had been allowed to choose his own time and was now having coffee and a private chat with Roxburgh Smith in the office.

Nairn stood at the window waiting for the familiar hunched figure to come round the corner, reflecting that if Carteret had a Soviet controller there had been plenty of time for him to take his, or her, guidance. And if he had made a panic contact that would prove his guilt, they knew nothing of it, for he had not been under surveillance, nor had his phone been tapped. He arrived half an hour later, walking slowly along the pavement from Curzon Street. No police, no guards, no danger of being destroyed like Penkovsky, even if he confessed to thirty years of treason. Alan Knight answered the door and took him into the room with hidden microphones.

Upstairs the other three in the team sat around the table

with the tape-recorders, each wearing old-fashioned head-phones. They heard Carteret and Knight sit down. A match was struck and they fell tense and silent as the questioning of their former Director-General began. 'Good morning, Jack. I take it the new DG explained that there are some allegations – allegations against *you* – that we'd like to clear up?'

'I know why you've called me here, Alan. I've nothing to apologize for, but I don't mind answering a few questions to help you, so long as it doesn't take too long.' His coolness was breathtaking.

Nairn made a few notes as Knight started to ask simple questions about Carteret's early life. Eventually they got to Shanghai and Knight asked why Carteret had left Oxford without a degree to go to China.

'To get away from the Church and my family.'

There was a silence. 'It was a long way to go just for that,' commented Knight drily. Carteret made no response. 'Did you know Agnes Smedley in Shanghai?' The question was abrupt.

'Oh yes, she was an American Communist. Very sociable, always giving parties for the international community – you could hardly miss her.'

'And Richard Sorge?'

'I suppose I ran into him – he was a well-known journalist, after all, as well as a Russian agent – but I don't remember anything specific. Of course I didn't know he was an agent then.'

'Did you know any other Communists in Shanghai?'

'I expect so, but I can't recall any names.'

'Conditions for the poor in China were appalling in the thirties and Chiang's Nationalists were just thugs and bandits. Communism must have seemed the only solution to many people?'

'Must it? I was working for British American Tobacco, didn't really think about it.'

'But you were a journalist before that – you must have thought about it then.'

'No, not really.'

'Are you telling me, Jack, that you – an intelligent man –

were there at the start of the Chinese Communist revolution and didn't even *notice* it was happening?'

'Mao didn't come to power until 1949, you know – that was eighteen years later. In Shanghai we were all more afraid of the Japs.'

'Who recruited you to the Communist Party?'

'No one. I have never been a Communist. I spent most of my working life resisting Communism.'

'You went to Moscow on the Trans-Siberian Railway while you were in China?'

'I went home to England that way in 1936, when I returned for good.'

'Why?'

'I was ill with tuberculosis and it was the quickest way of making the journey.'

The questions went on and on, through Carteret's failure to get into MI6, his determination to join MI5, on into the war years and after.

'A Soviet agent in MI5, code-named Alec, protected Klaus Fuchs while he betrayed the atomic bomb programme,' thundered Knight. 'Do you agree with that interpretation of events between 1941 and 1950?'

'Yes, I think I do.'

'And that betrayal gave Russia nuclear weapons by 1949, since when the balance of terror has dominated world politics?'

'A melodramatic way of putting it, but you could say that.' Carteret had a dry, flat way of speaking and was showing no sign of being rattled.

'Then who, pray, was this Alec?'

'When I was head of the service I initiated the investigation of Richard Fell.'

'You're saying that Fell is a traitor?'

'It was never proved.'

'But you believed it?'

'Yes.'

'You're quite convinced?'

'It was also possible that the agent was someone older, who'd been in the service during the war and retired or died, but my money was on Fell.'

133

'Embling was active in the case against Fell, so why did you have him transferred to SIS?'

'I thought a Gestapo was forming that would tear the service apart as it explored every failure – and he was the ringleader.'

'But there *had been* a lot of failures, Jack. The list of cases that went wrong is endless. Enemy agents always seemed to be forewarned when they were in trouble, especially Philby; and why were there no defections of Soviet agents in London, only in America and the Commonwealth?'

'I've no idea.'

'Some say it's because they all knew there was a traitor at the top of our service, who would betray them to Moscow?'

'Yes, I have heard that theory.'

At the end of the day Carteret took a taxi to Paddington, to catch his train back to Somerset. Simon and Nairn walked down to a pub called the Chesterfield in Shepherd Market. 'What do you think, Jim?' Nairn eyed his pint and drew on his pipe.

'We'll never prove anything like this – Carteret knows all he has to do is deny everything and keep talking to discover how much evidence there is against him. We aren't allowed to use watchers, or tap his phone or open mail, because Roxburgh won't go to Ministers to get clearance. He's afraid to confess that Carteret may have been a spy. Even if he broke, they'd prevent a prosecution. It's a bloody farce.'

As Nairn walked down the corridor to his office, he remembered that curious day sixteen years ago. They hadn't made the connection between Sonia and Alec then. If they had, they might have cleared or damned Carteret once and for all, then focused on officers he'd recruited personally and helped into the service . . . but as it was, he'd been dead within three years, leaving a morass of confusion and suspicion behind him; and it was still there.

27

Berlin

Sarah met Magda on the street corner near her hotel and
they went for a walk in the park south of the Tiergarten, to
avoid walls that might be bugged. She explained the approach to be used with Sonia, sensing that he was memoriz-
ing it step by step. Behind his bluff, beery façade, this man
was sensitive and intelligent. It was dusk, dark enough for
them to be anonymous when they stopped by a kiosk to buy
two hot sausages with thick, spicy mustard. They stood in
the shadow of some bare trees, feet scuffing in piles of
dead leaves. 'And how exactly,' growled Magda between
munches, 'am I supposed to get this lady of nearly eighty
out of my God-forsaken country? Particularly if she doesn't
want to go?'

Sarah sighed. 'With difficulty. The submarine is there
now, sitting on the bottom of the Baltic, a few miles from
Rugen. It can stay for days without detection, because radar
can't pick up its position under water, but it's in radio contact
with London. I don't know quite how – I think they float an
aerial on the surface to pick up ultra-low frequencies or
something.' Magda popped the end of the long *Wurst* into
his mouth without comment.

'Watchers from the Embassy – or employed by them –
will be outside when you confront her. The idea is that you
take her and Len to the coast in your car – straightaway, if
she'll go, otherwise twenty-four hours later. It has to be at
night. When you get to the Baltic, you make for a particular
beach that is a long way from any coastguard stations; I'll
show you where on the map. When you leave Berlin, the
Embassy will alert the sub. Four hours later it will surface
and send a boat in.'

'It's crazy, absolutely crazy.'

I couldn't agree more, thought Sarah. David's finally gone off his trolley. Instead she said: 'They say it will work.' Christ, how unconvincing she sounded. 'The boat will flash a signal and you reply with an infra-red torch.'

'I don't *have* an infra-red torch.'

'I've brought one for you – it's at the hotel. After she's on the sub, you should be back in Berlin before dawn. Okay?'

Magda tucked her arm in his and started back towards the hotel. 'Ingrid, my dear, it is true that Peter is under suspicion and that this reflects on his mother. It is also true that we have revived the rumours of the fifties – that Sonia was a double agent who betrayed Fuchs and the others.' He stopped and lit a cigarette; it glowed red in the dark. 'She is worried and nervous, but honestly I can't see it being enough.'

Sarah said nothing.

'It won't work, Ingrid. To make her defect will require the imminent prospect of jail or a bullet in the back of the neck. Without that I don't believe she'll go.'

'Are you refusing to do it?'

'No,' he groaned. 'I've done mad things for that tall Scotsman before and sometimes they've panned out. She might denounce me, but I think she has the sense to see that would only do her harm – to admit an approach from your people would just increase suspicion.'

Sarah did not speak, knowing that for this likeable, fat man the penalty for discovery would be appalling. He would pray for death long before it came. 'Why do you take these risks, Magda?' she asked quietly. 'Why? Why not just come and live in the West?'

She sensed his smile in the dark. 'I didn't like the Nazis, Ingrid, but then the Red Army came in 'forty-five . . . they were swine, animals, you can't imagine. I was sent with the Hitler Youth to fight them – I was thirteen and very skinny because there was no food, too skinny to be fighting tanks with a 1914 rifle and no bullets. When they had finished raping and murdering and burning the city and set up their puppet government, I had doubts about Marxism too . . .'

136

he laughed. 'My family were all dead so I became a thirteen-year-old comrade to survive; later I decided to fight the bastards.'

Sarah knew that the risks he had faced for twenty years required a deeper commitment or hatred than that, but this was not the time to pursue it. 'London wants her out, not you dead. If you don't believe the plan will work, I can tell them. There's no point in taking chances for nothing.'

'I trust your Scotsman – I'll risk it.'

'When?'

'Tonight. We can walk back to my warehouse – there are some points I must go over again with you – and then I'll return to the East. Will that give you time to alert the Embassy in Unter den Linden?' They had come to a busy street, bright with neon signs for bars and restaurants, and hurried across to the crowded pavement on the other side.

'Yes, that's fine.' She squeezed his hand encouragingly. 'I want to call at the hotel first in case there's a message from Olympia.'

At first he was numbed by the shock of being arrested. He felt terrifyingly impotent with his hands manacled behind his back and his grazed face and leg were throbbing; a trickle of warm blood oozed from his nose and he could not stop it by sniffing. After ten minutes he tried to stand up in the back of the swaying van, but when the wheels bumped over a pothole he fell heavily to the floor and burst into tears as he lay there, sobbing with fear and frustration.

When he stopped weeping, he struggled to his knees and managed to edge up onto the steel bench at the side of the van. The small barred window was dirty, but through it he could make out that they were driving swiftly through districts he did not know, past factories and tenement blocks, a railway marshalling yard and a barracks flying the Soviet flag, guarded by soldiers with Asiatic faces. He had thought they would go to an office in the centre of Berlin and was mystified when they reached the suburbs, passing villas in leafy gardens and patches of brown farmland.

Eventually the van slowed and turned up a bumpy track through pine woods, stopping in a clearing. After a long

delay, the rear door opened with a clang and he clambered
out awkwardly, pinioned arms painful with knots of cramp.
'Where are we?' His voice shook with terror as he eyed the
Schmeisser machine pistol pointing directly at his stomach.
'What are you doing with me? I *must* see someone in auth-
ority.' Sweat was pouring down his face.

The two guards said nothing, but one of them gave a
cracked smile. To his amazement he felt the handcuffs being
unlocked and instinctively rubbed his wrists to restore the
circulation. He stared at the two men in confusion, but
before he could speak again they seized his arms roughly
and started to run. He was dragged along between them
panting, protesting weakly, feeling his feet scuffing through
dead leaves and fir cones, almost falling when he tripped
over a tree root.

Suddenly the wood ended and he saw wire fencing and a
watch-tower about fifty yards ahead. On the other side of
the border was a canal and an American army jeep bouncing
along the towpath. In a wave of horror he saw the terrible
irony of what they were doing to him. 'No,' he screamed.
'You don't understand – let me explain!' But then he felt
a sickening blow on the shoulder and staggered forward,
regaining his balance to stumble in panic among the concrete
tank traps and coils of barbed wire.

The burst of bullets struck him like a whiplash, a sudden
line of white-hot pain piercing from his left shoulder to the
small of his back. He heard the explosions and the metallic
clatter of the machine pistol as the impact hurled him forward to fall on his face, choking as warm blood flooded into
his throat. His whole body writhed as he tried to escape the
razor slashes of agony, a sticky crimson pool spreading
beneath him, then slowly the pain eased into blackness and
silence.

28

London

The Flash telegram from East Berlin was on Nairn's desk and decoded twenty minutes after it had been sent. He sat alone in the darkening room, staring abstractedly at the roofs of South London through the window. The crunch would be tonight. Magda would confront Sonia late in the evening; and within twelve hours Nairn would know either that the fragile plan had worked, or that it had collapsed like a house of cards.

He had decided to stay at Century House all night, to deal with every report as it came in. He might spend an hour or two on the camp-bed in the room at the end of the corridor, but he knew that he would not sleep. Two radio operators were in the communications room across the passage and would work in shifts with two others throughout the night, sitting at the console with its computer terminals and shaded blue lights.

For an hour or two there would be nothing to do, but Nairn did not feel like turning to the routine files in his locked in-tray. He would go for a short stroll down to Lower Marsh and have a pint in the Spanish Patriot where he could be alone with his thoughts, for he remained uneasy about the whole operation. Nairn disagreed with Simon's determination to solve the Carteret problem at any price. Instinctively he had long been as certain as he wished to be of the answer and the attack on Sonia was distasteful. He also had a premonition that it was all going to go horrifically wrong. He had felt that premonition before over the years . . . and usually it had been right.

He was pulling on his shabby raincoat when one of the radio operators came in. 'Yes, Liz?'

139

'Mr Charlton is on the phone, sir, from East Berlin. Will you talk to him on the scrambler?'

Nairn looked puzzled. Charlton was head of station at the Embassy on Unter den Linden and had sent a cyphered telegram only half an hour ago; if something had happened since then, it could be nothing good. He picked up the green phone and spoke abruptly. 'Nairn here.'

'Are we on a secure line?'

'Yes.'

'Something has happened today, something that might bear on the operation.'

'Yes.'

'There was a shooting on the East Berlin boundary – a man trying to escape to the West at the fenced border south of the city. The frontier guards gunned him down, of course. He didn't stand a chance; I don't know why they go on trying, but it happens every day.'

'Who was he?'

'I am reliably informed that the victim was Peter Werner.'

'Werner? But I thought he had papers to leave via Czechoslovakia – and he'd promised to wait for a tip-off from you before he went?'

'That's what I thought too. Maybe he got cold feet.'

'The bloody young fool – he's dead, you say? No danger of interrogation?'

'He's dead. An American patrol saw him shot to bits.'

'Shit, this alters everything . . . has anything happened to Sonia?'

'I've got her apartment staked out with watchers, but nothing has happened so far. There's no sign of MfS people, which is a bit odd.'

'Is Magda still on the safe side of the Wall?'

'Yes, Cable's at her hotel in the West and Magda's nearby.'

'Okay, leave me to think for a few minutes. I'll contact Sarah through Olympia and come back to you, probably by telegram, so get ready for some instant decoding.'

In Adlershof, he lay in the dusty loft, looking across the street to the apartment block and listening to the device he

140

had planted weeks before, using an earpiece of the kind supplied with transistor radios. The signal was still beaming back to the recorders in the Embassy. Clearly Sonia and Len were alone in the apartment but he had heard nothing of interest for two hours, except one side of a telephone call in which Sonia had used only two words 'yes' and 'no', and had sounded frightened.

The windows of her flat were in darkness, except for one which he knew to be the living room. The street was equally dark, but lit at intervals by white lamps reflecting in puddles left by a shower of rain. Occasionally a car passed. One of his colleagues was in a Volga parked at the kerb, two others at the back of the building. There was no sign of watchers from the MfS, but he had a feeling that they were somewhere down there. Perhaps they were hidden as effectively as he was himself. He was still pondering this when two long black cars drew up at the kerb opposite. They looked like Russian Zils. Five men got out and entered the apartment block.

29

Berlin

Nairn's message changed everything. Sarah and Magda set off for the Wall with adrenalin flowing. A young man from the SIS office at Olympia had been waiting in the hotel lobby when Sarah went back for her final check, leaving Magda sipping a solitary lager at a pavement café. Hurriedly she took the messenger upstairs and listened to him in her bathroom with the taps running. Ten minutes later she and Magda were hurrying through the maze of alleys away from the bright lights. Gay West Berlin stopped well before the Wall. 'So the sonofabitch tried to cross the fence in the south?' Magda sounded suspicious. 'No wonder they shot him down. The bloody fool – why didn't he wait and use his papers?'

'Maybe he lost his nerve. He was shit-scared all the time he was with me.'

The policeman gave a growling laugh. 'I'm not surprised; but this makes everything so much more dangerous. Now the bastards will be on watch. God knows how I'll get into her apartment without being seen, let alone make it to the coast.'

'It will also make her realize how vulnerable she is. She'll run willingly enough after Peter's death – the little runt has ruined her.'

'Just so, Ingrid. Now the great plan of our lunatic friend in London might – I repeat *might* – conceivably work. But we haven't a moment to lose – her enemies must already be closing in.' The same growling laugh again. 'Very convenient that young Peter was so stupid . . . almost *too* convenient.'

They had reached the run-down tenements of Kreuzberg, breathing in the spicy cooking smells of the Turkish quarter.

It had grown dark and they were only one street from the greenish-white floodlights playing on the Wall. It was visible at every corner: a rough construction of breeze blocks about twelve feet high, covered in aerosol graffiti and occasional plaques where would-be escapers had died. 'It looks nasty and out of date,' muttered Magda. 'It *is* nasty, but not out of date. Nothing has changed in forty years – that's the enemy over there, even if no one likes to admit it.' He had stopped outside a derelict warehouse and glanced up and down the empty alley before taking out a key and opening a padlocked door.

Inside, the building was empty, its windows black and gaping without glass. Magda pulled out a torch, which showed the concrete floor covered in rubble and splintered timber. Sarah coughed in the cement dust that fell from the roof as the door was closed. The white beam probed ahead, reflecting in two luminous green eyes that scuttled away noisily. 'A rat,' grunted Magda. 'There are hundreds of them. Mind where you step, the whole place is falling down.'

'How do we cross the Wall?'

'Shades of Harry Lime. There's a manhole down into a sewer in the yard, we paddle through the shit and come up the other side.'

'It can't be that easy.'

He laughed. 'The sewer tunnel is blocked by a steel gate, but I have the key. It helps to be a major in the *Ministerium für Staats-Sicherheit*.'

'How do you get back if you lose the key?'

'There's a spare one taped to the underside of the manhole out there. Okay?'

'You'd think they'd block it up permanently.'

'Why? There are dozens of little tunnels that cross under the Wall – even the U-bahn for the West runs under East Berlin at one point. It's convenient for both sides to have ways of crossing unobserved.' He paused. 'Well – wish me luck, Ingrid. It's tonight or never for our Sonia. Don't forget to close the padlock on your way out.'

'Good luck, Magda, but why can't you bring Sonia out this way, without all the palaver of the submarine?'

'Because the sewer lets you out in the closed zone the

other side of the Wall. It's illegal to enter without authority – as a security officer I can go where I please, but she'd be stopped and arrested.' He kissed her and turned towards a door into the dark yard.

The crash was deafening and sent a volley of concrete splinters raining down from the roof like shrapnel. Sarah covered her head with her arms, crouching for protection and choking in the dust. When she opened her eyes she could see nothing but darkness. She felt for the small but powerful torch that was usually in her pocket; thank God it was still there. Its light showed that her clothes and skin were covered in a deposit of grey powder. Magda had vanished. She crawled forward to the edge of the pit where the floor had collapsed, the splintered remains of rotten boards sticking out a few inches from its sides. The floor creaked and sagged beneath her.

She spread her legs apart and reared up from the waist, to throw her weight away from the edge, then shone the torch down into the hole. It was an old well shaft. Magda lay at least fifty feet below. His head was crushed by a concrete beam and the twisted body partly covered in rubble. There could be no doubt that he was dead.

She drew back calmly: she felt sick but this was no time for emotion. Magda was dead and it was already late in the evening. If she went back to the hotel the operation would be aborted and no one would blame her. She stood up cautiously, hearing more debris fall down the shaft, then sat on an empty wooden crate.

There was no point at which she made a conscious decision. After a minute or two she stood up again, skirting round the gash in the floor, and found the door into the yard. The manhole cover was hinged and lifted easily. Below was a round brick shaft about four feet in diameter and a steel ladder. A stained holdall was jammed between the top of the ladder and the brick wall.

Sarah sat on the edge of the shaft and opened the bag in the light of her torch. It contained a pair of East German car licence plates made in thin plastic, a screwdriver and a nest of small spanners. Magda must have hidden them there, ready for this operation; she knew that Sonia had a car, an

144

old Lada. She untaped the brass key, put it in her pocket and ran over the possibilities once more.

It would be easy to go back and leave someone to make the decision . . . but that would mean failure, for tomorrow would be too late. She was not afraid and knew enough tradecraft. She was carrying her Austrian passport and the infra-red lamp was in her pocket. Sarah shook the dust from her clothes and descended the ladder, closing the manhole cover behind her. At the bottom, the sewer was high enough to stand up, with a steel walkway along one side of the tunnel. The stream of water was flowing quite fast and the smell was not too bad. But which way to go?

She chose the direction that seemed to point towards the Wall. Five minutes later she was rewarded by the sight of a heavy steel grille blocking the tunnel. The torch beam picked out the brass padlock that hung on the other side and a red notice headed *Achtung!* warned West German sewer-men not to go further even if the gate were open.

She left the gate unlocked in case she needed to come back in a hurry and advanced into the Soviet zone, carrying Magda's holdall. After about three hundred yards, there was another steel ladder rising into an access shaft. She wiped the dust from her face with a handkerchief and pulled up her skirt to shove the plastic number plates down her tights, resting against the sides of her thighs. The tools and street atlas went into the pockets of her raincoat and the holdall floated away on the stream.

For the first time she began to feel apprehensive as she climbed the ladder, until her head touched the steel of the manhole cover. There were no hinges, so she placed both her hands under it, took a deep breath and lifted.

30

London

After he had sent his telegram to Charlton, Nairn poured himself a whisky and lit a pipe. He knew the instructions had arrived and there would be no more phone calls unless something went wrong. Although calls could be scrambled, he was sure the lines were tapped and an increase of traffic between Olympia and London would make the East Germans suspicious. He smiled wryly: as if they didn't have plenty to be suspicious about already.

Peter's death had changed the odds, which Nairn hoped were now marginally in his favour. Even so, the plan could fall apart all too easily. Sonia might sit it out, a stray bullet from a border guard could take her secret to the grave . . . the albatross could stay around the neck of both services. Looked at coldly, after forty years of betrayal and suspicion the possibility of an end seemed almost unreal. He spread a street plan of Berlin on his desk, but his mind wandered inexorably to the messy conclusion back in the seventies.

They had recalled Carteret for a second day of interrogation, but Roxburgh Smith had put a clamp down after that. Even if the man had been a spy, a total of about ten hours questioning was unlikely to reveal it. However, Carteret had a heart condition and his successor was mindful of John Watkins, the Canadian Ambassador to Moscow who had been suspected of treachery a few years earlier. After twenty-six days of questioning in Montreal, his interrogators were convinced of his total innocence, at which point he had died of a heart attack while still facing them. The Carteret case was too bizarre, too threatening to risk that kind of tragic publicity.

Carteret returned to Somerset, played golf and continued

as a member of Bridgwater Rural District Council. Impotent investigations went on even after his death from a heart attack in October 1973, but that had been the end for Nairn. He heard the news on a day when he was already preoccupied: it was the fifth anniversary of his wife's death in a car crash and his memories of Margaret were still very precious. Simon had telephoned and suggested they go to Carteret's funeral. Nairn had agreed without thinking.

They had driven to Somerset on a bright autumn day. Catcott was a curious mixture of old sandstone and modern houses. The church was small and pretty, with a barrel-vaulted roof and rough-hewn country pews in a whitewashed nave. Like Great Rollright, so well chosen by Sonia, it had seemed curiously isolated, despite being close to biggish towns like Taunton and Bridgwater, but Nairn had dismissed the comparison as fanciful.

After the service they had passed the dead man's cottage while looking for a pub. It was small and run-down, washed dull pink with a red pantiled roof and long overgrown garden. Somehow it seemed an odd place for a powerful man to retire: bleak, dull, almost eerie. But if he was a traitor fleeing from the truth, perhaps it was ideal? Or was he just old and ill and tired of being falsely accused after doing his job – whatever the failures – as well as he could for thirty years?

It seemed indecent to go to the village pub, so they stopped at the Knowle Inn on the road to Bridgwater. Jim Simon was still drinking pints in those days and Nairn ordered two, wondering – not for the first time – whether Carteret and Fell might not both be innocent men: framed by the Centre and crucified by their colleagues, to protect a wartime traitor long since dead, or someone else still in place.

The green telephone buzzed and Liz told Nairn that Olympia was calling. 'They shouldn't be, I ordered silence.'

'It's on scramble, sir.' Nairn pressed the button and heard a man's voice. 'It's Bill Charlton again, Sir David.'

'What the hell is it this time?'

'I wouldn't call, but it's about Miss Cable.'

Nairn started.'Yes?'

147

'She's vanished.' The voice sounded uncomfortable.

'What do you mean "vanished"?'

'Went off with a mutual friend of ours about seven o'clock and didn't return to the hotel as planned . . . I suppose she might have gone off for a drink or something?'

Nairn knew there wasn't the slightest chance of that; Sarah was on duty and if she hadn't returned something serious had prevented her. 'Thanks for telling me. Check the obvious places where she might be and let me know if there's any *definite* news, good or bad. Otherwise maintain silence until tomorrow.'

He put the phone down and groaned. Just when he had thought he was winning, it was all falling apart.

31

Berlin

There was a moment of panic when she lifted the grating, but her courage returned when she found her eyes level with the cobbles of an alley that was empty and in darkness. Sarah climbed the last few steps, replaced the manhole cover and walked briskly towards the lights of a street. As Magda had said, she was in the barren area behind the Wall and she passed a police post, but no one challenged her. Thankfully she was going in the wrong direction to cause suspicion and her belted raincoat had a military cut to it in the dark.

The street plan was in her pocket, but she knew it by heart. This was the Leipziger Strasse and if she walked eastwards she would cross the River Spree and come to the Alexanderplatz; but before that she would turn right, along the Spree Kanal, for the S-Bahn station at Jannowitz bridge. The walk took about ten minutes, through streets darker and emptier than those in the West.

At Jannowitz she crossed the river, hurried boldly into the station and bought a ticket. Adlershof was eight stations to the south-east. The line divided at Ostkreuz, and the first train to arrive was going north to Pankow. The second was okay – destined for Schönefeld airport outside the city in the south. She took a seat in a half-empty carriage and hid behind the newspaper she had bought on the bridge.

Sarah reached Adlershof at eight forty-five and turned into the neat residential area between the S-Bahn and the series of narrow lakes through which the Spree flowed on its way out of the city. The streets were lined with comfortable-looking villas and apartment blocks. The plan she had seen at Edge had been accurate down to the position of bus-stops

149

and she followed it to Friedlander Strasse. She knew which apartment block was Sonia's and where in it her flat was located, but to avoid any hostile watchers she could hardly enter by the front door.

She walked slowly along the street, under the trees on the opposite side to the apartment block. Other buildings jostled it on both sides and there seemed only narrow gaps between them. Sarah continued to the next corner, turned right and right again, until she was in a narrow service road running along behind the buildings; as she expected, there were high-walled yards with garages and parking spaces.

The street lamps were widely spaced and dim, so she felt comfortably invisible as she backed into the shadow of a wall. There were no parked cars and no people in sight. She hurried along in the dark, counting the buildings, until she reached the block before Sonia's. There was a dark space behind it, where several cars were parked: they all appeared to be empty. Boldly she turned and walked into a brightly lit door, up a few stairs to the front hall; one wall was covered in steel mail-boxes. She pressed the button to call the lift, tensing as a woman in a drab overcoat came through the glass street door carrying a briefcase.

They entered the lift together. The woman pressed the button for the third floor and Sarah the one below the top. The woman nodded to her vaguely but said nothing. When the lift stopped a second time Sarah, now alone, sent it on up to the top floor and stepped out.

She was in an empty corridor of modern red doors leading to apartments. At the end was a door with an illuminated sign over it showing a drawing of stairs and the words *Notausgang*; she reached it in three strides. The emergency staircase was in darkness, but the battery of her torch was holding out and she followed its beam up to a grey metal hatch, which opened easily when she pulled down its long handle. She was on the roof. Putting out the torch, she waited until her eyes became accustomed to the darkness. There was a little moon slanting through breaks in the clouds. The roof was flat, but wet and slippery, surrounded by a low parapet and criss-crossed by large pipes. At one end was a chimney for the central heating boiler. Crouching low, Sarah climbed cautiously over the first pipe and then two more until she reached the end of the building. The roof of Sonia's apartment block was about four feet away, with a slightly higher parapet, several chimney stacks and the undulations of old-fashioned tiled ridges.

She looked down into the well and felt sick. If you fell those eight floors you would break half the bones in your body and, hopefully, die on impact; the alternative was too appalling to contemplate. But the gap was only about four feet. Surely she *could* jump it, despite having to start from standing still on top of the parapet?

She climbed on to the low wall, swaying, willing herself to look straight ahead and not down. The number plates in her tights made her move awkwardly, so she stepped down again, took them out and threw them across. They landed with a soft plop. Next she took off her raincoat, bundled it up and threw it too, followed by her shoes, which made a scratching noise as they slid down the tiles. She took off her tights, tied them round her waist and hitched up her skirt to leave her legs free.

She climbed on to the parapet again, gripping with her toes, crouched to tense the muscles of her calves and thighs – and sprang into space. Her eyes closed in a moment of total terror, but then she felt her left foot grazing stonework and toppled forward to break her nails clutching a slope of tiles. She had landed with a thud, but guessed that it was not loud enough to be heard below as she lay spreadeagled on the roof, feeling her heart pound painfully in her chest.

When she was dressed again, she crawled along the gulley behind the low wall that edged the roof, tearing her tights and scraping her knees on rain gutters and sharp joins in the lead. At the back she found what she was expecting. This was an older block with no emergency stairs inside but an iron fire escape spiralling down the wall. She checked the time with her torch and decided to rest for half an hour. Ten o'clock would be about right.

It started to rain again as she climbed down the iron staircase, slithering on the wet metal, pressing her body into the wall for invisibility. At each level there was a balcony running to either side of the steps, with doors opening on to it. Sonia's flat was on the fourth floor. There was a half-glazed door, the room behind it in darkness, but pressing her nose against the glass Sarah could see that it was a kitchen with an internal door ajar and leading to another room. She took a deep breath to steady her nerves.

The kitchen door was locked. If it had security bolts she would have to break a window. Tentatively she probed between the door and its frame with a piece of plastic the size of a credit card. It was easy, the tongue of the old-fashioned lock slid back, she pressed the door gently and it creaked open. There was no more time to think. She took off her shoes and crept through the kitchen, opened the door abruptly and entered the living room.

It was empty. The curtains had not been drawn and grey light filtering in through the windows showed a large room with a shadowy circle of armchairs round a fireplace. Sarah froze and listened, but there were no sounds of life, just the swish of a car passing on the wet street outside.

Holding her breath she tiptoed across the room and opened the other door. It gave on to a dark corridor. She flashed the torch and gingerly opened the row of doors one by one. There were two bedrooms, a bathroom and the front door, which she left closed.

One thing was clear. The flat was deserted. Sonia and Len had gone.

32

London

Nairn stood at the window, staring down grimly at the dark streets of Lambeth. So it had all gone sour. According to Olympia, Sonia and Len had been taken away by men in plain clothes, presumably from the security police, about three hours ago. Looking for Sarah, Charlton had gone to Magda's warehouse and found his body. Nairn was sure Sarah had gone under the Wall in his place, but God knows where she was now.

He cursed. He should never have sent her back to Berlin – and now there was nothing he could do to help her. Absolutely nothing. Of course he would make a scrambler call to the Embassy in East Berlin and get hold of the head of station, but what could they do? Put a few people on the streets? Keep an eye open? Pray? The chances of them finding Sarah were remote; and even if they did, it would be hellishly difficult to get her out again.

Reluctantly he looked up Simon's home number in Dorking. There was nothing useful Simon could do either, but the sooner he was warned of impending disaster the better. If Sarah was caught and identified there would be political ructions, as well as personal grief.

After the first shock, Sarah wanted to weep at finding her quarry gone. Her nerves were in tatters after the tension of the last two hours – and all for nothing. But then she pulled herself together and sat down in the dark living room, trying to calm her fears. At least she was safe enough for a bit: Sonia's apartment was the last place anyone would think of looking for her. She looked around, shielding the torch beam with her hands. It was a comfortable flat, quite big by

East German standards. There were crowded shelves of books and an old-fashioned, tiled fireplace, its mantelshelf supporting holiday snaps of children and a photograph of a youngish man in a silver frame. That must be Richard Sorge.

What should she do now? If Sonia had been arrested, Sarah ought to get back into the West as soon as possible. She would be stopped at any of the checkpoints, for she had no papers to be in East Berlin, but she might be able to find the sewer again. That would be okay if she wasn't picked up in the zone behind the Wall, and if no one had found the gate open . . . leaving it open had been a mistake. If these efficient Krauts found a barrier down, they probably closed it with a new padlock. Damn, damn, damn!

Alternatively, maybe Sonia was still at liberty. They were an old couple, retired: they might be so upset about Peter that they were staying with one of her other children. It was still only eleven o'clock – they might just be out for a meal, though that seemed unlikely if they knew Peter had been shot. Maybe he wasn't dead after all and they'd been allowed to visit him in hospital. Sarah went to the window and peered out. The street was empty, except for a single car parked under the trees on the other side. Could be a watcher. Friend or foe?

It was the car that decided her. It was very late and all good East Berliners were in bed. She would be conspicuous in the streets and, if that car were from MfS, she'd be picked up before she had gone a hundred yards. Suddenly she felt enormously tired – and safe in the dark womb of the apartment. She found a can of beer in the fridge and drank it in the smaller of the two bedrooms, which was furnished with a single divan. Then she wrapped herself in a blanket, curled up and went to sleep.

33

London

Sir James Simon did not hang about; nor did he stand on ceremony. He caught the first train from Box Hill and hurried on foot from Waterloo Station to reach the Cut by seven in the morning. After a tussle with the security guards – for he had forgotten his pass for the building – he was admitted and taken up in the lift.

Nairn greeted him warmly enough, but looked grey with fatigue. 'You're up early, Jim – thanks for coming in.'

'Is there any news?'

'Not since we spoke. Sarah Cable is somewhere in East Berlin – God alone knows where. Sonia has vanished. I don't know whether she's been arrested, but since her son appears to have been shot while trying to cross the border, it's certainly possible.' A clerk brought in two mugs of instant coffee with sachets of powdered milk. 'Sorry the commissariat arrangements aren't quite what you're used to.'

Simon gave a slight, self-deprecating smile. 'It seems to be a complete failure.'

'It's a disaster. If East German security arrests Sarah and she admits to being an SIS officer, who has entered the country illegally to abduct Sonia, God – all hell will break loose.'

'And what about the old woman?'

Nairn spread his arms wide. 'Who knows? She's got reasons enough to defect now, even at her age, but I suspect she's no longer in a position to do it. For all I know she's already locked up.'

'I doubt it.'

'And we've still got this bloody submarine sitting on the

bottom of the Baltic. Shall I tell the Navy it can go fishing?'

'Leave it for another twenty-four hours; they agreed to wait two nights and it's only been one so far.'

'It seems about a week.'

Simon sat down in one of the shabby armchairs. 'Do you think they really will arrest Cable?'

'It's a distinct possibility.'

'Then I'll have to make a report to Ministers; they hate being caught with their trousers down.'

'Is that strictly necessary, Jim? It means an awful lot more people will know. Sarah seems to have stayed free so far, but a leak might put every Vopo in East Berlin after her. There's a hell of a lot of flappy ears around the Sovbloc embassies, all only a phone call away from Karlshorst.'

'David, when things go wrong I *have* to make a report to the politicians. There's no alternative.'

Sarah woke to a sunny autumn day and an apartment that was still empty. Keeping well away from the windows, she made coffee in the kitchen. Curiously she did not feel like an intruder any more; the place had a sympathetic atmosphere and she felt almost at home. When she peered cautiously through the bottom corner of a window, kneeling on the bedroom floor, she saw a quiet residential area outside, streets lined with trees. She could also see a few passers-by and parked cars. If the apartment was under surveillance, any of those might be watchers.

She assessed the situation calmly. Whatever might have become of Sonia, there was no reason to believe that East German security knew that she, Sarah, was in East Berlin. Ergo she would be safer in the empty flat than on the streets in daylight. Ergo she should stay there all day, until evening and darkness, then leave the same way that she had arrived. With luck she could take the S-Bahn back to the centre and get as far as the British Embassy without being stopped. There had to be some official way they could get her out after that.

She was tempted to try her luck straightaway, but there was no way of avoiding watchers in daylight, and she was not afraid of the police coming to the apartment. If Sonia was in trouble, it was because of Peter; no one in his right mind was going to suspect Sonia herself of anti-state activities, so there was no reason for them to rummage her home for evidence. They could get at her without that.

Anyway, the apartment had two exits. The front door had a spy hole, through which Sarah could see a stairwell and an old-fashioned lift. The back door from the kitchen led to the balcony and the steel fire escape. The balcony was about a metre wide, with a solid brick parapet, so that if need be she could crouch there unseen from below. Sarah left the door to it unlocked and slightly ajar, in case she needed to use it in a hurry.

Since the place might be bugged, she could not turn on the radio or television to pass the time. Instead she examined the books in the living room. One was a faded German volume about Richard Sorge's wartime exploits as an under-cover agent in the German Embassy in Tokyo. Sarah knew of this as a classic piece of espionage – Sorge had seen that the secrets of the Japanese High Command reached Moscow as quickly as they reached Japan's allies in Berlin. This intelligence had told Stalin that Japan would not invade Russia, enabling him to turn all his forces against the invading German army. As a reward, he had refused to exchange Sorge for Japanese prisoners and left him to be hanged in the last year of the war. She settled down in an armchair to read.

Late in the afternoon the heat came on and as the room grew warmer she dozed in her chair. She was woken by a scratching noise. Sitting up abruptly she heard it again. It was the front door being unlocked.

She thrust the book out of sight under a cushion and fled to the kitchen, crawled through the outer door, so that she would not be seen from below, and crouched on the balcony. Her throat went dry with fear as she heard footsteps echoing inside the apartment.

34

Berlin

After about fifteen minutes, a combination of cramp in her legs and spitting rain began to make Sarah restless. She peered cautiously through the kitchen window and saw an elderly woman going to a cupboard. The woman was speaking to someone in the next room and Sarah listened. She heard the name 'Len' and deduced from the tone of the conversation that the couple were alone.

It was time for the final gamble. She made her decision, counted to twenty, opened the kitchen door and turned the radio on loudly. 'Good evening.' Sarah spoke quietly in German; no microphone would pick her up under the racket from the transistor. 'Don't be alarmed. I mean you no harm – I have come from London, to save you.'

Sonia started and turned round, a look of sudden terror in her eyes. 'Who are you?' She shrank back. 'What do you want?'

Sarah held out her hands to show that they were empty. Sonia looked no older than her late fifties, a handsome woman with short white hair, a face full of wisdom and character. 'What do you want?' Her voice trembled. Sarah noticed the twisted gold of an oriental ring, that must have been on the old woman's hand for half a century. Her husband ran in from the other room and put his arms round her protectively.

'You're in trouble, aren't you?' demanded Sarah. 'Both of you. I have come to help. May I sit down?'

Len nodded; he had a kind face and looked as if he had been weeping. 'They shot Peter,' he said to Sonia. 'The girl's right, whoever she is, we are in terrible trouble. You've been sixty years in the Party and they treat you like this.'

'Peter's death was an accident,' replied Sonia, tightlipped. 'It does not place you and me in any danger.'

Her husband stared at Sarah desperately. He seemed to accept her presence, showing no surprise at the sudden appearance of an uninvited stranger. 'We've been questioned by the security police for twenty-four hours. Suddenly, after all these years, we are suspect, just because of Peter – God knows what they will do to us.'

'We are in no danger,' Sonia spoke again in a monotone, as if still in a state of shock.

Len groaned. 'Face it, Ruth, for God's sake face it.' He turned to Sarah again, his eyes pleading. 'Whoever you are, can you do something to help? *Please*.'

It was an hour later. The radio was still blaring out Beethoven and the old woman eyed Sarah warily across the kitchen table. Sarah felt a wave of despair. At first she had felt that she was getting somewhere; but now she could not risk staying much longer. Sonia would not budge. 'You're wrong,' Sarah said quietly. 'I tell you again – you aren't *wanted* here any more. It doesn't matter what you did when you were young, you've opposed repression, spoken your mind, made enemies.' Sonia stared at her in silence. Deep down, surely she must be upset about Peter, she must be bitter and afraid; but there was no sign of it. In desperation Sarah tried again. 'For God's sake listen to me,' she wanted to scream. 'They believe you were a double agent from 'forty-seven to 'fifty, that you *betrayed* Fuchs. Your son has tried to defect. If you stay here they'll disgrace you, expel you from the Party, take your home and lock you up with criminal lunatics! Don't you understand? You may spend the rest of your life in jail. We are offering you a way out.'

Sonia glared at her malevolently, then suddenly dropped her eyes. 'What are you trying to make me do?' She was still trying to sound dismissive, but no longer quite succeeding.

'We can get you out of the country. We can do it *tonight*, then offer you both a home in Britain or America, wherever you want.'

'In exchange for betraying everything I have worked for these last sixty years?'

'That's better than staying here to be destroyed – *isn't it*?'

Sonia's face darkened, but her resistance was flagging. 'And just supposing I would submit to this blackmail – exactly *how* would you propose to get us out?'

'The Baltic coast is only a hundred miles away and a submarine will be waiting at a certain time tonight.'

Sonia shook her head sadly. 'Just like the war . . . but it's impossible, my dear. There are coastguards and patrol boats, radar and mines – no one could get away like that any more.'

'We have studied the details and timing of patrols and our Navy can spot mines. I promise you we *do* know how to do it, and it's been done before. One can always get away by sea, you know that from the past.' Sarah paused, then smiled and pressed on almost casually. 'So are you going to try?'

'I don't think so; I was just warning you of the dangers if you were going to try yourself.'

'Very well,' Sarah sighed and felt like spitting blood; she had no more cards to play. For the first time she noticed that there was a photograph of Sorge in this room, too: a small, faded black and white print on the dresser. 'I can't stay here all night. If you prefer to remain and take your chance, too bad, we can't help you. But I don't believe you'll be living together in this apartment in a week's time. And that will be just the start.'

Suddenly Sonia's face crumpled. 'Oh, *why* can't you leave us alone? All I want now is to live quietly with Len, in the socialist country I helped to build, among people who speak my own language. Oh God, why must you torment us – leave us alone, you *bastards*.' She had started to cry, sobbing quietly with her head in her hands.

'The world has changed since 1950 and the country you helped to build is one where young men you despise will condemn you as a traitor.' Sarah's legs were trembling under the table, but her voice was firm and echoed away into a hollow silence.

Eventually Sonia looked up with eyes full of anguish. 'Please leave us alone for a little while – I have to talk to my husband.'

*

160

They left at midnight. Sonia insisted that Len should not share the risk of escaping from the north coast. 'There is no need. He has a visa to cross into West Germany, because he was going to a trade fair in Hamburg in a few days. He was going to cancel the trip because . . . because of Peter. But he could still use the visa; it was really me they were questioning, so I don't think he will have problems at the border if he travels by train.'

Sarah had her own doubts, but kept quiet; her job was to get Sonia out, whatever might happen to poor Len. 'But *you* would be stopped?'

'Oh yes. I have no documents to leave the country and now they'd be watching for me – it has to be your way.'

'How can we get out of this apartment block without being seen?'

Sonia had drawn a blind over the kitchen window, but now she pulled it back a few inches and peered out. 'A little tradecraft.' She still looked haggard, but gave a sad half-smile. 'The service road at the back provides no cover for watchers, so they will be at either end of it. At the front, I'm sure they are in a parked car.'

'Where is *your* car?'

'That's what I was thinking. It's a Lada, can you drive it?'

'Certainly.'

'Ah,' Sonia shook her head. 'I forgot. It has special Party licence plates – if they are watching for me they'll spot us at once.'

So that was why Magda had made the false plates. 'I can change the number,' said Sarah. 'And I have papers for a Lada to match the new one.'

'Do you? Now that *is* clever . . . then perhaps we *can* do it. My car is in a lock-up garage a block away. I rent it on the black market and I'm sure the police don't know; they will assume our car is in a garage at the back, but there are too few there for all the occupants of this building. Socialist planning.' She paused wryly. 'If you can get the car, drive back here and along the service road at the back. They are looking for me, not for a girl in her twenties in the wrong car, so no one will challenge you. Then stop in the dark behind the block, in the entrance to our yard, and I'll slip

161

in and lie on the floor in the back of the car. With luck the watcher on the other corner won't give you a second glance.'

Sarah hesitated. 'But how do I get to this garage?'

'I'll show you on a street plan. To get out of the building go down the stairs to the basement, which is at ground level – the front door is up a flight of steps from the street. There's a side door. Go into the yard and you can walk along the *back* of the next apartment house, then through an alley and along the *front* of the one after, where you'll be concealed by the shrubs in the garden.' Sarah chuckled inwardly: she was dealing with a professional. 'At the end of the street you just cross over and walk away. Here, let me show you.'

'Is there enough fuel in the car?'

'Yes, the tank is nearly full and there are maps for the whole country.' Sonia gave another sad smile. 'A habit from the past.'

The yard was dark and Sarah felt her way carefully past the large, wheeled garbage containers. It took ten minutes to reach the row of garages three streets away and she saw nobody on the way; if there were any watchers, they were well concealed. Sonia's garage was the seventh in a row of eight near a Gothic building that looked, surprisingly, like a church that was still in use, for outside was a neat signboard giving the times of services.

Sarah unlocked the garage and slipped inside. She pulled the wooden door closed quietly, using her plastic card to hold back the tongue of the lock. There were no windows, but instinctively she shielded the fading torch with her hands as she knelt on the concrete floor. The licence plates of the square car were fixed on with small nuts and bolts, which she attacked with her screwdriver and the tiny nest of spanners. She put on the replacements with the same bolts, pushing them easily through the thin plastic that had been used to make them. When the job was done, she concealed the old plates between the rafters and the corrugated asbestos roof, then opened the door a few inches and stuck her head out. The street was in darkness, except for pools of white light around two concrete street lamps, and still appeared deserted. Gingerly she unlocked the car and started the engine. The noise sounded deafening and she switched off hastily, before it attracted attention or carbon monoxide filled the garage. She opened the garage door and ran the car out, anxious to keep this dangerous exposure to a minimum. Within a few seconds the doors were shut again and she was passing the silent church on dipped headlights.

She gripped the wheel of the strange car tensely, driving as if in a trance, but it all went smoothly. She turned into the narrow street behind the apartment block, veered into the black yard and had barely stopped when she heard Sonia open the rear door.

'The pick-up point is on the coast near Rugen,' Sarah said briskly as they accelerated. 'Can you direct me to the autobahn round the city?'

'Yes,' came the muffled voice from the back. 'Turn right at the next corner, then go on for about ten kilometres, until we come to a tram terminus.' They were driving swiftly along an empty street, past dark rows of shops and apartment houses, occasionally bumping over tram tracks or patches of cobblestones. Sarah sensed that Sonia did not want to talk and concentrated on the strange controls, watchful for police cars. Deep down she knew that she was terrified: one mistake and they would be finished. Whatever happened to Sonia, Sarah would be in for a long spell in a hard regime prison or labour camp; they would break her health before they exchanged her, they always did. But on the surface all she felt was a curious, nerveless calm. At the tram terminus they turned into an area of forest and picked up speed.

In London Nairn was still alone in his office, motionless at the desk with its green-shaded lamp. It was one in the morning and he had just deciphered another short telegram from East Berlin. The Embassy's watchers had reported the departure of a Lada car, driven by an unidentified woman. And now Len, too, had left for an unknown destination. There was nothing to do but hope; if he had kept the faith of his Quaker parents, he would have prayed.

35

East Germany

There was no autobahn to Rugen, but in any case Sarah felt safer on the winding country roads. She drove north through the night at a steady fifty miles an hour, white headlights probing the darkness of the pine forest. From time to time the trees gave way to heathland or marsh, and when there was moonlight she could see the ghostly outlines of farmhouses.

Once clear of Berlin, she stopped in a lay-by and Sonia came to sit beside her. They drove on in silence, speaking only when Sarah checked the direction at road junctions. There was little other traffic: they passed a few eight-wheeled trucks pulling trailers and a solitary Vopo on a motor cycle, going in the opposite direction. Sarah's spirits lifted, confident as they covered thirty-five miles in the first hour. Then the fog came down.

It was quite sudden. Ragged bands of grey mist appeared in the headlights, obscuring the road and sweeping up over the moving car like phantoms; then they were facing a solid wall of fog and Sarah was forced to slow to a crawl. 'Are there foglights on the car?' she asked Sonia.

'I'm sorry, no.'

Sarah cursed but pressed on cautiously, peering ahead to spot the edges of the road in her dipped headlights. There were no helpful cat's-eyes and she switched on the wipers to clear the haze of moisture from the windscreen. They whirred back and forth noisily. The next hour was nerve-wracking, for if she hit a tree or drove off the road they were finished. But Sarah also felt reassuringly invisible in the fog and they were comfortable enough with the heater blasting out hot air. She gripped the wheel tighter, leaning forward in an effort to see, her forehead touching the glass of the screen, her eyes beginning to ache with the strain. They passed through a town, its buildings mostly obscured by swirling mist, tyres drumming on cobbles and headlights picking out cars parked in the street. 'This must be Neubrandenburg,' muttered Sonia tensely. 'Be careful.' But there was no sign of the Vopos and no challenge.

Soon afterwards they left the fog behind and Sarah picked up speed again. Now they were crossing flat heath, the road was wider and soon she was doing sixty, trees and telegraph poles flashing past in the darkness. It was Sonia who saw the roadblock ahead, suddenly clutching Sarah's arm with a gasp of fear. A row of red lights showed a barrier placed across the road and two jeeps standing beside it. With nothing but open country to each side, there was no way of escape. As the cluster of uniformed figures drew closer, Sarah braked and wound her window down. Two men in long greatcoats approached, both carrying sub-machine guns.

In London Nairn was back in the communications room, drinking a cup of cold instant coffee. For two hours there had been radio silence and he was expecting no further news until he heard from the commander of the submarine – and that should not be until Sarah and Sonia had been picked up safely. He chatted to the radio operators about children and gardens: he had neither of his own, but they were both family people, whom he had known for many years. His thoughts were elsewhere and he barely noticed when a telephone warbled and the woman he was talking to paused to answer it. He turned away and watched the lights of the traffic coming down from Westminster Bridge. It was thinning out now; by four o'clock the road would be empty. As night workers all over the world knew – police, nurses, customs officials, street cleaners and intelligence officers – that was the dead hour when even insomniacs and would-be suicides slept, when all life seemed to pause with exhaustion before deciding to struggle on for another twenty-four hours.

He realized that the radio operator was speaking to him. 'Yes, Liz? Sorry, I was miles away.'

165

'It's GCHQ, sir. They have a report you should see –
sounds like it refers to tonight.'

'Yes?'

'They're sending it up on the secure FAX, should be with
us in twenty minutes.'

'Okay, make sure I get it straightaway.'

'Of course, sir.'

Sarah stared up at the broad, high-cheekboned face below
the military cap, terrifyingly aware of the muzzle of the gun
pointing directly at her head. She could see from the man's
face and the shoulder-boards on his greatcoat that he was a
Russian soldier, not a Vopo, and when he spoke she could
not understand a word.

She shook her head and he raised his voice, gesturing
angrily with the barrel of the Kalashnikov. 'It's all right,'
whispered Sonia. 'He is asking us to wait a few minutes.
There are military manoeuvres going on and a squadron of
tanks will cross the road just ahead of here.'

'Is that all?'

'Yes, don't worry.' Sonia leaned forward and spoke a few
words in Russian. Suddenly the Asiatic face grinned, the
soldier turned away and marched back to the barrier, sub-
machine gun hanging loosely across his chest. Sarah saw
him in conversation with the other troops. A bottle passed
between them and there was laughter as the soldier made
an obscene gesture towards the car, thrusting his forearm
and clenched fist into the air like a rampant penis. Sonia
took her hand gently. 'I think he liked the look of you, my
dear, but there is nothing to fear. They are just drunken
peasants and will do us no harm.'

It was not a few minutes but over half an hour before the
tanks came. Sarah heard a distant rumbling, then engines
roaring deafeningly as they rose up from the east. It was an
awesome sight, at least fifty armoured monsters – surely
more than a squadron – with long gun barrels and waving
radio aerials, bucking across the heath at high speed. Sarah
watched in fascination as their steel tracks clattered across
the road; it was like a flashback to the Second World War.

Then they were gone, the barrier was raised and the two

jeeps set off in pursuit of the tanks. Sarah started the engine again.

The report from GCHQ was devastating, though half expected. They had finally made sense of the whole series of intercepts and Nairn swore quietly as he read them. Why the hell had he been so blind? Why had he been so crass as to send Sarah back? She was a brave girl, but only twenty-two – what would those bastards do to her? And if there was shooting when they picked them up . . . 'Fuck,' he shouted to the empty room. 'Fuck, fuck, *fuck*.' He beat his fists on the desk in frustration.

After a few minutes he walked in a trance to open the door and called across the corridor. 'Could you get a car standing by, please, Liz? I may need to move quickly when we finally hear something.'

'No need, sir,' said the radio operator. 'Your own driver's waiting downstairs. He's been there all night.'

'Chris is still here? But I told him to go home hours ago.'

Liz appeared in the corridor. 'Perhaps he thought you might need him, sir.' She grinned conspiratorially. 'It's a big one tonight, isn't it?'

'Ay, it might be.' More likely Chris was clocking up a gold mountain in overtime, thought Nairn; he wasn't known in the canteen as Chris the Crook for nothing.

At three fifteen in the morning Sarah hit the coast near Greifswald. After the tanks the journey had been without incident, but she sighed with relief when the car breasted a hill and she saw the faint spiky outline of the sand-dunes ahead. The Baltic showed up as an expanse of darkness a little less black than the land, flecked by pinpoints of silver where waves were breaking.

She slowed and turned along the coast road, knowing that it would be some miles before the dunes gave way to shingle and low cliffs, where hopefully she would find the ruined watch-tower that marked the pick-up beach. They were now entering the most dangerous phase, for this isolated coastline was one of the most closely guarded in Europe, but Sarah felt curiously calm and confident in the darkness as she listened to the splash of waves and smelt the ozone blown in from the sea.

36

Rugen

After concealing the car in a thicket of trees, they crouched
on the shingle for the best part of an hour, sheltering between
two rocks from a bitter wind. Fortunately there was no
longer any moon and Sarah felt secure in the blackness at
the base of the cliffs. She sat hugging her knees, staring into
the dark at the ghostly shapes of white breakers crashing on
the shore. Sonia sat close by and Sarah sensed that she was
weeping silently. She reached out and put her arm round
the old woman's shoulders. They said nothing, but there was
a silent bond between them. Finally Sonia spoke. 'It is an
end.' Her voice trembled and was barely audible. 'I can
never come back here, back to my home, again.'

'I'm sorry.' Sarah felt inadequate, but went on hugging
her, trying to comfort.

'Do you think Len will be safe?'

'I hope so . . . yes, I'm sure he will be.' Sarah wished that
she believed it.

There was another long silence, broken by the crash and
hiss of waves on the shingle. Suddenly Sonia whispered:
'Why did you come to Berlin? You never explained . . . we
just accepted you as a saviour. But who sent you?'

'I came from London, where they knew about . . . about
Peter and thought you might need help.'

Sarah sensed that Sonia's eyes were staring at her in the
dark. 'But that's not *all*, is it? It can't be so simple, nothing
ever is. What do they want from me in return?'

Sarah hesitated. Her instructions were not to press Sonia
for information, just to get her safely out of the country.
Even so, think of all that wasted effort if the old woman
died of exposure before they reached the submarine, or was

carried off by a coastguard's bullet; and suddenly she seemed willing to talk. 'I suppose they want to hear about the past, when you were an active Soviet agent.'

'When I was in England, perhaps?'

'Maybe – I'm not really in the picture, you know. I'm just helping you escape.'

'But you must know *something*, I think . . . is there anything particular they want to know? Any one *vital* thing?' Sonia was no longer trembling and there was a sudden hint of mockery in her tone.

Sarah stared at the darkness in silence. 'They want,' she said deliberately, 'to know who you controlled in MI5 during the war. Who was it that protected you when you ran Fuchs – and then went on to become a top man in our Security Service? Who betrayed the whole set-up, lock, stock and barrel, to Moscow in the sixties?' There, it was out. If she'd blown it, it was too late to go back.

'Is that all?' Sonia gave a light laugh. 'All this fuss and danger, just to discover that . . .?' The irony hung in the air.

'Yes, that's all. Alec was the code-name.' Sarah gripped the old woman's arm fiercely. 'Come on, Sonia! I'm risking my bloody life to get you out of this God-forsaken hell-hole of a country, so for Christ's sake who was Alec?' For a moment her voice rose angrily above the roar of the sea.

Sonia shook herself free. 'Stop hurting my arm, girl. I and others in the KPD dreamed of a socialist Germany from the end of the Great War. Rosa Luxemburg died for it in 1919, when the Spartakists tried to rise in Berlin, before anyone had even *heard* of Hitler . . . all those years in China and England I longed to return and give my life to creating this God-forsaken country as you blindly call it.'

In her anger Sonia had snapped back into German and Sarah replied in the same language. '*Entschuldigen*, I'm sorry. I didn't mean to offend you.'

'No matter, you are still very young. Tell me, what is your real name?'

'Sarah.' She told the truth and paused, waiting for truth in return. 'But look, my question was serious. We do need to know – *who was Alec*? It's not a lot to ask for all the risks we're taking.'

'Isn't it? Perhaps not . . .' The same hint of mockery again. 'Very well, Sarah, since you are so anxious to know, and I am so old, and we may both shortly die of frostbite in this wind, I will tell you something about Alec.'

The old man sat on a bench on the station concourse, waiting patiently for his connecting train to Hamburg to appear on the indicator. Although it was so late, a few other passengers dotted the platforms: most in drab winter coats, a little group in army uniform. A Vopo in a long military greatcoat was patrolling to check papers. When he came to the elderly man with the tired, sad face below the white hair, he examined his passport and visas cursorily. 'Where are you going, then, grandad?'

'To Hamburg.'

'And what is the purpose of your journey?'

'I'm going to a trade fair for my factory.' Len gave a wink and a cynical little chuckle. 'I still have to work even at my age, you see, much as I wish it were otherwise.'

'We are building for the future, grandad.'

'So we are, young man, so we are.'

Once again Nairn crossed the corridor to the communications room, with its dim view across the river to the Houses of Parliament where the floodlights had been turned off hours ago. Inside, he was in turmoil, but struggling to maintain a calm front, to stop his fingers drumming restlessly on the window-sill. He studied the pattern of street lamps, broken up by the red and white lights of moving cars on the bridge, before turning to the middle-aged woman at the console. 'Anything else come in, Liz?'

'No, sir. The sub is still out of contact so I suppose it's sitting at periscope depth.'

'It's worrying – they should have picked them up by now.'

'I expect it will work out, sir. The landing party was SBS, wasn't it? They'll get them off if anyone can.' Nairn wished that he shared her optimism.

*

171

It was nearly four in the morning when Sarah saw the pinpoint of light far out in the bay. It flashed twice. She pointed the infra-red lamp and switched on two long bursts and a short one. She hoped to God they had the right night-glasses to see it. 'They're coming,' she whispered, clasping Sonia's arm in reassurance. Then she needed both hands for the lamp, keeping up a steady series of long and short flashes invisible to the naked eye. No one was going to see anything from the land behind them. From time to time the black clouds parted to reveal a patch of star-strewn sky, but mostly the darkness remained impenetrable.

It was a shock when she heard a soft scraping sound, followed by splashes and the crunch of boots sinking into the pebbles. A narrow patch of deeper blackness rose to block out the grey of the waves; and Sarah started as she looked up to see two men in front of her. They were wearing black wetsuits and balaclavas; even the patches of skin around their eyes and mouths had been painted black. Both carried machine pistols. One bent forward, peered at the huddled figures of the two women and whispered in an unmistakable Welsh accent: 'Frau Beurton?'

'Yes – and I'm Sarah Cable. Thank God you're here.'

'Cable? No one told me about you. There's supposed to be a poofter copper who's going back to Berlin.'

'I'm from London. I've brought Frau Beurton here and I'm coming out with her.'

He examined her face in the dim blue light of a torch and seemed satisfied. 'Okay. I'm Sergeant Evans. Can you both stand?'

'Yes – we're perfectly all right.'

'Good, then follow us down to the boat.' Sonia looked back at the cliffs and hesitated; but then they were slithering over the shingle, the two women hand in hand, escorted by an armed man to each side. At the water's edge a third man was holding a large rubber dinghy. They lifted Sonia bodily into the boat and Sarah scrambled after her, feeling the water icy on her legs as a wave swept in and the inflatable reared up to float free. The men rolled over the side in a practised way and two of them started to paddle vigorously out to sea.

172

'Put these on,' ordered Evans, proffering two anoraks with linings of a soft, warm material. 'Then lie in the bottom of the boat. It's bloody cold out there.'

Sonia wrapped the anorak around her small frame. 'Thank you.' She turned and stared at the black coastline, the lights of a town on Rugen glinting away to the right. There was a low popping sound and Sarah realized that an outboard engine had been started, muffled in a kapok-lined box at the stern. The boat started to move fast, bucking in the swell, and they all lay in the bottom, except Evans who crouched up to steer. They would be almost invisible on the surface and would not show up on the radar; the only dangers were meeting a coastguard cutter or hitting a rock or floating wreckage. The lights of the town disappeared. Sarah was glad that they were already out of sight of land, but several inches of cold water were slopping about in the bottom of the inflatable and, as it rolled sickeningly over a high wave, she began to feel queasy.

Suddenly she sensed the vibration of the outboard fade and raised her head; they were still moving and the spray whipped her face, but the muffled sound of the engine had ceased. 'Get down,' hissed Evans.

'Why are you stopping?'

'Just bloody get *down*!' Then she saw it: the black shape and red starboard navigation lamp of a patrol boat about two hundred yards away, a pool of dim yellow light from its wheelhouse outlining the long gun on the foredeck. 'Oh God,' her throat went dry and she cursed inwardly. 'Have they seen us?' The only answer was a hand pushing her head roughly below the rubber side of the boat; she felt Evans lying rigid beside her and the chilly steel of his pistol against her face.

37

London

The radio operator took off her headphones, rubbing her eyes with tiredness, and turned to Nairn. 'That was Northwood, sir. The submarine was due to radio in at seven minutes past four if they *hadn't* made contact with our people on the beach. If contact had been made, the commander's orders were to maintain radio silence until they're on board and out of East German territorial waters. So they must have picked them up by now.'

Nairn smiled wanly. 'Any chance of Northwood missing the signal from the sub?'

Liz, an ex-Wren, grinned. 'You must be joking, sir. If there was no signal, the plan *must* have worked – congratulations! Why don't you go and get some shuteye now?' She still spoke as if she were a young Wren in the ops room at Portsmouth, despite the passage of twenty years and bringing up three children.

He looked sceptical. 'Thanks, I hope you're right. I've got to leave shortly, but I want to know the moment you hear anything from that sub.'

'Of course. I'll ring you at home.'

'I'm not going home, but for the next few hours you can get hold of me on this number.' He scribbled on a pad.

Nairn left the building twenty minutes later, after making a series of scrambled phone calls. The Rover was waiting outside with the engine purring and he was glad to find the heater on, for the air struck cold after the warmth upstairs. He settled in the left-hand corner at the back of the car.

'Where to?' asked his driver cheerfully.

'Are you sure you're fit to drive, Chris? You can't have been to bed for over twenty hours.'

'Had a kip in the security guards' room, thanks, sir. I'm fine. *You* look knackered.'

Nairn grinned in the dark. 'Okay, Chris, go north to Marylebone Road and take the A40. When you get to High Wycombe on the M40, wake me up.' He was asleep by the time they passed the old Admiralty building in Whitehall, his head resting awkwardly against the glass of the car window.

Len's train stopped with a jerk a mile before the West German border. An elderly Skoda with police markings bumped across a ploughed field, white beams from its headlights waving drunkenly in the dark, until it reached the embankment close to the locomotive. The two Vopos seemed to know which carriage to go to and mounted the steps deliberately. Len accompanied them with no resistance and the train started again as the three men drove away into the night. A few passengers watched and shook their heads sagely: probably an escaping criminal or a fool trying to cross without papers. Most of the train was unaware that anything had happened.

Sarah and Evans peered over the rubber bow as the engines of the patrol boat faded and its navigation lights grew smaller in the distance. 'I think she missed us,' he sighed in relief. 'Thank God for that.'

'But it was *terrifying*.' Sarah ducked as a wave splashed into her face. 'Was it accidental – or are they looking for us?'

'Christ – how should I know? But it was too damn close for comfort.'

'How much further to this submarine? It's getting awfully rough and it feels like we'll soon be in Sweden.'

'We're only a few miles offshore, Miss Cable, but I think we're almost at the rendezvous point.'

'How the hell do we find it?'

'With great difficulty. I've been trying to follow a compass bearing from the coast and they're waiting at conning-tower depth on that bearing. I have a little electronic bleeper to help them spot us.' He studied his instruments in the light of the blue torch, shielding it with his body, and moved aft. Sarah heard the soft putter of the engine again. The boat picked up speed, but the waves were bigger now; every time they reached a crest they plunged into the trough with a sickening jar and icy water poured in over the sides. Whenever Sarah looked up the spray lashed her cheeks painfully. Her bare hands stung with the cold, but she picked up a plastic bucket and started to help the two men who were already bailing. She had read about this kind of thing in files: snatching agents from the beaches of Bulgaria or the Baltic States. On paper it sounded easy, but the reality was appalling.

Sonia lay inert in the bottom of the inflatable and Sarah prayed silently that she would survive the wet and cold. This was an insane way to rescue someone of nearly eighty and, as another wave soaked her up to the waist, she felt certain that they would all soon sink without trace. But Evans' navigation was better than he had suggested and after another ten minutes Sarah felt a surge of relief at the unmistakable dark outline of a submarine, floating boldly on the surface about a quarter of a mile ahead. The hull was partly submerged, its bow and stern awash, but the conning-tower alone looked huge.

'Okay,' snapped Evans. 'We're going to make it. When we get there I'll run the boat right up on the deck. Bill, you go first with the German lady – straight down the hatch just for'ard of the tower. Then you, Miss Cable – and for God's sake be as quick as you possibly can. Every minute she's on the surface, the sub's exposed to their radar and we're in danger. Understood?'

They crouched in tense silence as the inflatable bounced on over the waves. The submarine grew larger, rolling slowly like a long steel whale, cataracts of white water pouring down her sides as the foredeck rose from the sea. Sarah was helping Sonia to kneel up, ready for the jump, when she heard Evans curse. 'Oh shit, *shit*. That bugger of a coast-guard's coming back!' The clouds had parted again and there was enough grey moonlight to show the huge bow wave of the East German patrol boat returning at speed; the roar of diesels rumbled across the water and a searchlight suddenly pierced the darkness.

After a flash of horror, Sarah tried to calculate the odds. The patrol boat was coming straight at them and the submarine was still hundreds of yards away. Although the outboard was driving them forward fast, she knew instinctively that they were finished. She cursed in frustration as the beam of the searchlight slowly traversed the choppy waves, coming inexorably closer, and a guttural German voice started to crackle through a loudhailer. It was impossible to make out the words, but a burst of machine-gun fire followed. 'Lie down!' screamed Evans. 'Get right down. We can still make it, we're almost there!'

Sarah lay flat in the water slopping on the rubber bottom and put her arms around Sonia protectively. 'Are you okay?' she whispered.

'Yes.' The answer came with a chuckle. 'Isn't it exciting? Quite like old times.'

To her amazement Sarah felt a jerk and realized that they had beached on the steel deck of the submarine. Perhaps they would get away after all. She knelt up and saw Evans leap out into knee-high water as the great ship dipped slowly into the swell. Seizing the painter he jerked the boat backwards to a higher, dry section of deck, where a hatch was opening and heads peered out. 'Come on – jump!' he shouted. '*Now!*'

At that moment the whole world burst into white flame. The patrol boat was only a hundred yards away and its searchlight beam had focused on them with savage accuracy. Sarah was blinded as she struggled to help Sonia out of the inflatable, then deafened by the loudhailer and the clatter of the machine gun. She ducked as bullets clanged against the conning-tower and ricochets whined overhead.

'Jump!' shouted Evans again, his face contorted with strain as he clung to a deck grating with one hand and to the rubber boat with the other. 'For Christ's sake, jump!' One of the other men was kneeling and firing back in rapid bursts, trying to put out the searchlight.

Still struggling to help Sonia, Sarah stood transfixed by the blaze of light; she felt the old woman sway to collapse on the steel deck. With a shriek of pain the kneeling man dropped his Armalite and toppled over the side. Then the machine gun turned on Evans and Sarah hurled herself flat as bullets hammered murderously into his flak-jacket. Evans staggered backwards, releasing the boat to clutch at a wound spurting blood from his neck. Sarah grabbed wildly at the rubber as it slid away from her. The bow of the submarine dipped again and a massive wave washed right along its foredeck. Sonia vanished and Sarah screamed in terror, blinded by salt as the freezing water knocked the breath from her lungs and swept her into the sea.

38

Great Rollright

It was nearly dawn when Nairn drove into the village. The Rover crept past the ghostly shapes of trees and houses, as the first shaft of cold mauve light probed up behind the Chilterns. Chris stopped the car on a patch of waste ground and Nairn sat back exhausted. He felt horrible inside; apart from the strain of the operation, he had eaten nothing for twelve hours and the smoke in his lungs stung like mustard gas. He ought to give up that filthy pipe. He pulled on his raincoat, for it was bitterly cold, and set off down the lane in the half-light. Except for a herd of cows, shuffling noisily at a gate in the hedge, Great Rollright was asleep.

The Firs lay in darkness – how was he going to wake her? But when he turned into the yard behind the cottage, he was relieved to see a dim light in the kitchen. Nairn tapped gently on the back door. There was no response and he turned the handle. The door was open; he doubted if it were ever locked. The flagstoned scullery was in darkness, but yellow light shone through a crack where the door to the kitchen was ajar. He felt his way through the jumble of bicycles, toys and miniature wellington boots and tapped again; but still there was no reply. When he opened the door he stepped back in amazement. It was Sonia, kneeling in the corner, transmitting to Moscow. Then he realized it was the foster mother, crouching with her back to him as she fiddled with a large short-wave radio. The kitchen was hot, warmth flooding out through the open doors of the range, and she wore only a nightdress. The indentations of her spine and the soft swell of her buttocks were outlined firmly against the thin white cotton.

Nairn coughed and she turned round, her eyes startled.

'Good God, what on earth do you want at this time in the morning? Keep away from me!' She stood up sharply, staring with fear, her arms across her breasts as if she were naked. 'Oh, it's *you* again; but isn't it just a bit bloody early to come calling?'

'I'm terribly sorry if I startled you, I know I'm barging in.'

'You are rather. The hour between six and seven is the only time I get to myself. I like to listen to the BBC World Service when I've raked out the stove, while I do my aerobics.' She grinned mischievously. 'Five minutes later you'd have found me cavorting about in my leotard or worse.'

'Worse?'

She giggled; the shock had quickly gone. 'Sometimes I do them with nothing on. Lots of people do if they're alone – where *have* you been all your life?'

Automatically she filled a kettle, placing it on the range, hissing where the water had splashed down its sides. She sat down, pulling her nightdress closed as it fell open to reveal the firm curve of a thigh; she might live alone with the children, in conditions of near-squalor, but Nairn noticed that she shaved her legs. Last time her shapeless working clothes had concealed her body, but now he could see that it was not only her face that was beautiful. He put her age at about thirty-eight, but she looked younger.

She smiled and swept a long tangle of auburn hair back over her shoulder. 'I'll make some tea when the kettle boils. Did you actually *want* something, or were you just passing by at six in the morning?' She raised her eyebrows archly.

'What's your name?'

'Alison. Alison Wragg. *Mrs* Wragg. The kids call me "dishrag", which is no doubt a fairly accurate description most of the time. That's why I cling to my hour of health and beauty every morning. But I'm not doing it in front of you, it's private.' She got up and made tea in the huge enamel pot.

'I didn't know you were married, Mrs Wragg.'

'Alison. I'm a widow.'

'I'm sorry.'

180

She shrugged. 'My husband drowned six years ago, along with our son – they were sailing in a dinghy. We were on holiday in Cornwall.'

Nairn leant forward and touched her arm. 'I'm sorry. That must have been awful.'

She smiled at his touch and did not pull away. 'Yes, it was rather.' She poured two mugs of tea. 'I was teaching in a unit for maladjusted children in the East End of London, he was a GP in the same borough. We were very happy. After the accident, I chucked it all up and came down here.'

'So you're really a teacher?'

'*And* I trained as an educational psychologist.' She had a wry, humorous smile. 'I always wanted to be a doctor like Tom, but they turned me down. When he died I thought of going back to my maiden name of McKenzie – people do tend to joke about a name like Wragg, you know – but it seemed disloyal. I really don't know why I'm telling you all this.' The eyes in the gentle face narrowed. 'Or perhaps I do – you're terrifyingly easy to talk to. I suppose you know that. You frighten me.'

'Am I? I'm really quite harmless – you don't need to be frightened.'

'Don't I?' She crossed her knees again and this time the leg stayed bare, but it was not a feminine wile – she was unconscious of it, her whole attention focused on Nairn. 'Look, I may not be all that bright, but I'm not a complete cretin. So stop playing with me. Who the hell are you and what, if anything, do you want?'

'I'm *not* playing with you.' He paused, pondering his selection of worknames, but he was not going to lie to her. That leg was long and quite brown, must be from working in the garden, he couldn't imagine her sunbathing. 'My name is David Nairn and I'm from the intelligence service, what some people call MI6. I'm here because we need your help. It's important and urgent, otherwise I wouldn't be here at this hour of a morning.'

'Now, do I believe you? Have you got an identity card or something?'

'No, but you can call the police to check if you want.

181

I shan't be offended – they'll vouch for me and send a policewoman to chaperone us if you like.'

She gave a ribald chuckle. 'Chaperone? Good grief, I can look after myself, thanks. But you lied to me before – you said you weren't from the police.'

'I'm *not* from the police – and *you* lied to me.'

She started and went crimson. '*Did* I? How? I certainly didn't mean to.'

'I showed you some photographs – you said they were of Peter Werner, the Beurtons' younger son who visited you. But they weren't, were they?'

'Oh no, what have I done? Show them to me again.'

Nairn produced an envelope and spread the prints out on the kitchen table. She stared at them sightlessly. 'You can't see them, can you?' he said gently.

She shook her head. 'No, my sight isn't very good and I desperately need some new glasses – there just hasn't been time to get them. I'm sorry, I don't like to admit I'm getting old; I know it's silly. Have I done something dreadful?' She began to cry.

'You're not getting old. You're beautiful.' She smiled at him through her tears; the myopic eyes were a vivid blue. 'You just need some new spectacles.' He pulled out a small magnifying glass and handed it to her. 'Can you see his face with this? *Really* see it?'

She peered at the photographs and nodded. 'Yes I *can*, I really can. I'm sorry I messed you about.' She moved the glass over the prints and stared at them intently. 'But why did you say they were Peter Werner? It's nothing like him. Nothing like his brother, either.'

'Look again, please. This time we have to be quite sure. *Why* isn't it Peter Werner?'

'It just isn't. Peter is slim with dark hair. This fellow's nearly bald.'

'Could it be Peter grown older?'

'No, my dear. The eyes are different, the ears are different and the mouth is narrower. Those things don't change with age.'

'But are you *certain*?'

'Yes, quite certain.'

'Thank you.'

Ten minutes later the Rover stopped at the rusty metal gate into the churchyard. It was now light and a blue sign named the church as St Andrew's. Nairn skirted the flint wall of the chancel, walking down the slope through the grave-stones.

It stood in an overgrown corner, a square slab of granite, quite plain except for the inscription:

BERTA KUCZYNSKI
born 30 June, 1879
died 10 June, 1947

mother of
Jurgen   Ursula
Brigitte Barbara
Sabine   Renate

R R KUCZYNSKI
born 12 August, 1876
died 25 November, 1947

For Ursula, he thought, read Ruth, now Sonia. Fifteen years before he had never bothered to visit the grave, but at least it was there. Even the Centre couldn't have fixed that, so the story was true up to 1947. He shivered in the bitter wind: it wasn't true now. The man who had claimed to be Peter Werner was an imposter; Nairn trusted the woman called Alison and he was sure that the three Kuczynski children who'd visited her over the years had been genuine. Peter was a phoney, yet he had been killed, poor bastard, to authenticate his false identity. There was some terrible, momentous deception here – and he sensed the chess-player's mind of his old adversary Kirov behind it. He'd rumbled her just in time, but what in God's name was she trying to do? If Peter was a phoney, was *Sonia* genuine? Fancifully he wondered whether she had died and been replaced as well; but surely that was too ambitious? So what the hell was going on? He turned as he heard a shout from the gate. Chris the Crook was standing there, waving. 'Sir David. A call for you on the radiophone.'

39

London

The meeting was in Committee Room A at the Cabinet
Office, on the third floor at the back, looking down into the
garden of 10 Downing Street. Nairn had been there so often
that he no longer noticed the fine moulded ceiling and Adam
fireplace, only the uncomfortable green leather chairs. At
eleven-thirty coffee was served in an adjoining room, so that
the messengers who brought it – two middle-aged ladies in
blue overalls with brass crowns on the lapels – should not
see the papers on the table. Simon drew Nairn to one side.
'Alexander is waiting in my office, David, may I drag you
away?'

They hurried through twisting corridors to the Whitehall
side of the building. Sir William Alexander looked old and
ill, but the Director-General of the Security Service was not
due to draw his pension for another six months and was
determined to stay to the end, despite the cancer spreading
through his body that might well get him first. He was sitting
hunched at the conference table in Simon's office and did
not get up when the others came in.

Simon closed the door firmly and sat in the carver chair
at one end of the table; Nairn sat opposite Alexander, who
eyed him malevolently. 'I understand you've been monkey-
ing with skeletons in the cupboard of *my* service, Nairn?'
Alexander still spoke with patrician loudness, but his voice
was hoarse and his breath carried the unmistakable smell of
the inner decay of a dying body.

'On my instructions,' intervened Simon breathlessly.
'David has done only what I asked – and he was most
unhappy to be involved.'

Alexander's watery eyes pierced through the

co-ordinator: a thousand years of Anglo-Saxon pride dismissing the upstart Jewish immigrant. 'Then you should not have asked him, sir – and you are both responsible for what has happened.' His lip curled. 'It's a complete bloody shambles.'

There was a strained silence. Simon opened a file purposefully, as if that might solve something. 'I invited you here to put you in the picture, Bill.' The tone was well-modulated as ever, but his Viennese accent became more pronounced when he was rattled. 'There is no question whatever of interference in your domain, but I was asked to investigate this case by Ministers – and that is precisely what I have done.' He paused for emphasis. 'Perhaps, David, you would just run through the basic conclusions for us?'

'Surely.' Nairn turned to a typewritten report on the table in front of him. 'The starting point is the long-standing suspicion that Jack Carteret – or possibly Richard Fell – was a Soviet penetration agent while working at the top of Five. The case has been unsolved, and troublesome, for the last fifteen years. Since Ruth Kuczynski, code-named Sonia, appeared to have run whichever one of them it was during the war, the possibility of her defection from East Germany, after being invulnerable for thirty-five years, seemed a heaven-sent gift.

'Unfortunately, the whole thing rested in deception. One of her sons – now a scientist in the Democratic Republic – was spirited away to a long training course in Russia and kept incommunicado for months. An imposter, using his identity, offered to defect in San Francisco. We fell for it, and started to lean on his mother to come out as well.'

'When did you realize he was a phoney?' growled Alexander.

'I became suspicious soon after I first sent Miss Cable to meet the man calling himself Peter in East Germany. I picked up an intercept that puzzled me; it was less than half decyphered, but it was going to East Berlin from someone in their mission to the UN in New York and implied that they knew about Peter. I panicked about Cable's safety. Then more partial decrypts came in and it seemed that there was no danger, that Peter had been sussed but – although it looked a bit odd – he'd be allowed to defect without interference.'

The dying man made a gesture of contempt. 'Is that *all*?'

'No, Sir William, that is not all. Later – and now I fear it may have been too late – I went to Sonia's old house in Great Rollright and found that the real Peter had visited the place a few years ago. He'd been allowed to visit England for some sort of electronics course. Although he left the country with his mother only a jump ahead of the Special Branch in 1950, nobody in Five seems to have noticed him come back.' Nairn paused meaningfully and Alexander looked away. 'But he turned up on the doorstep almost in tears at going back to what he saw as his real home.'

'Why the hell should we have noticed?'

'Because Great Rollright was plainly an important time, and an emotional place, for the whole family. Both Sonia's parents are buried in its churchyard.' There was another strained silence.

'So?' asked Simon quietly.

'So the woman who lives in the house now remembered what he looked like. I showed her photographs of our Peter Werner, né Beurton, and she didn't recognize him. It wasn't the same man. I guess whoever dreamed up the whole scheme didn't know he'd loved the place so much, let alone that he'd go back there.'

'And you say the real Peter is in Russia?'

'According to my contacts, he's on a long course in Novossibirsk, safely tucked away for a few months. I'm sure he knows nothing of this.'

'If the son was a phoney, how do we know that the *mother* is real?' demanded Alexander.

'Nothing can be certain. It's possible that she's dead, or has also been spirited away, with her place taken by an East German agent; but I don't think so. I think she's genuine enough. She was a fine agent and deeply committed, so it would make sense for her to take part in a classic disinformation operation like this.'

'Disinformation?'

'Yes, that was the objective. After the first intercepts we managed to get some bugs and directional mikes on her apartment in Berlin. The HVA and others, presumably Russian, visited her there and told her to let herself be persuaded to co-operate, then to deceive us.'

'In what way?'

'That was never clear from what we heard. Carteret and Fell were never mentioned by name – if they had been we might have found the answer without all the hassle of getting her to defect. But she was briefed away from the flat on what to say to us – they took her to an office in Karlshorst by car.'

'But she was supposed to convince us that either Carteret or Fell – whichever was in fact innocent – was the traitor?' asked Simon deliberately.

'Just so.'

'Which must mean they still have good reason to protect the guilty man, even if he's dead. They *must* be muddying the waters to protect a successor.'

Alexander looked down at the table. 'It *could* make sense,' he conceded grudgingly. 'But she must have been barmy. All that drama on the high seas, risking her life – why should she do that at seventy-six, just for the bloody Party?'

'Because she *believes* in the bloody Party,' snapped Nairn. 'It's been her whole life for sixty years – and there wasn't supposed to be any risk. It was clear from what we overheard in Berlin that she was expecting to talk to us there, never leave her apartment.'

'That figures. Why did it change?'

'God knows. I think at the end someone decided that it would look more credible if there was a little more drama . . . perhaps it was always planned that way and they hadn't warned Sonia. She was very shocked when the Peter stand-in was shot and just went along with it when they told her to let Sarah take her as far as the coast. She was bounced.'

'David thinks Kirov may be the architect of the operation,' interjected Simon. 'And that finishing touch would be characteristic. Ruthless – but brilliant.'

'Who the hell is Kirov?' spluttered Alexander.

'First Chief Directorate and one of Centre's deputy chairmen.'

Alexander snorted as if he had known all the time and

turned to Nairn. 'If all this stuff is true, just how far were Sonia and Cable *intended* to get?'

'So far as I can tell, they were supposed to be stopped on the coast near Rugen, then "arrested" and separated. Sonia would have vanished and they'd have conned us into exchanging someone for Sarah – maybe the GCHQ man, he must have another twenty-five years still to serve. Then Sarah would have come back to us with the name Sonia had given her and, after all this effort and agony, we'd have believed her.'

'The culmination of forty years deception,' breathed Simon.

'But it didn't work!' Alexander's hollow cheeks quivered with fury. 'And where's Sonia now? Where's the girl? Where's the blasted sub, come to that?'

'I don't know the answer to any of those questions.'

'You don't?' Alexander broke into another fit of coughing. 'Then you damn well *should*. Let me just tell you something, Nairn. Five has never been your service and I'll move heaven and earth to make sure it never will be. My God, what a cock-up.'

The time was an hour earlier in East Berlin and the young man arriving at Schönefeld airport was slim and dark. The journey from Novossibirsk had been tiring, but uneventful. Even the two-hour wait in Moscow had been more comfortable than usual now that they were improving the terminal.

He had left his car at the airport and now drove straight home, where he left his case, then on to his parents' apartment in Adlershof. He had not planned to go there, but – as he would explain so often later – he had an uneasy premonition that he should. He parked the red Skoda in the street and walked back to a stall, where he bought a small bunch of flowers for his mother, then ran briskly up the four flights of concrete stairs. It was supposed to be good for the heart, but he was sweating slightly when he rang the door bell. There was no answer. He rang again, a long metallic jangle that echoed round the landing.

At the third ring, another front door opened and a

middle-aged man looked out sharply; Peter did not recognize the face. 'What's all this row about?' he shouted. 'Some of us have to work nights and are trying to sleep!'

'I am looking for Herr and Frau Beurton.'

'Can't you see they've gone away? Clear off.'

'They said nothing about going away – and I'm their son.'

The man shrugged. 'Everyone who comes says they're a relative. I don't believe it any more. Anyway the man from the housing department said the apartment is being reallocated.'

Peter Werner's face went white with shock. 'But where have they gone?'

'Um Gottes Willen, how should I know? That apartment was far too big for two old pensioners anyway. Maybe they've gone into a home, or been arrested,' he leered. 'Or one of them has died – they're old enough.'

'But –'

'But nothing. Bugger off or I'll call the Vopos!' He vanished back into his apartment and slammed the door.

In Moscow it was another two hours earlier and Major-General Kirov eyed the wet pines outside her modern office on the ring road with distaste. She preferred the architecture of Peter the Great, the wide squares and Western atmosphere of Leningrad, where she had been born Nadia Alexandrovna Kirova nearly sixty years before. Grey-haired with a round, apple face that had once been beautiful in a high-cheekboned Slavic way, she was still a handsome woman. Elegant in a well-cut suit of blue tweed, her movements were feminine, despite her use of the masculine form of her surname, a symbol she had adopted when fighting with the Viet Minh in Indo-China in the forties.

A male secretary knocked and entered through one of the high double doors that separated the office from the ante-room. 'The Bulgarian colonel is here, Comrade General.'

Kirov smiled. 'Then show him in, please.'

40

London

In a mood of deep dejection, Nairn caught the tube back to Lambeth North and walked the few hundred yards from the dingy station to Century House. He took the lift to the top floor and was gloomily unlocking the door of his office when a figure shot out of the communications room. It was the same radio operator as last night, the bouncy ex-Wren: must already be time for the night shift to come on again, the inexorable flow of life continuing.

'Sir David!' She caught his elbow excitedly.

He gave a bleak, questioning smile. 'Yes, Liz, what is it?'

She handed him a pink flimsy. It was a decoded signal from the submarine commander, timed at eleven that morning and giving a position in the North Sea off Denmark. *East German defector Beurton and escort Cable safe and on board. Two SBS other ranks lost when intercepted by GDR patrol boat. SBS Sergeant Evans wounded in sick bay. Await instructions.*

'Good God.' Nairn started to laugh, seized the blushing clerk round the waist and waltzed her down the corridor. 'After all that it worked! Kirov *has* scored an own goal, hasn't she?' Liz stared at him in puzzlement. She had never heard of Kirov and she had never seen Nairn laugh before.

The submarine docked in the Clyde twenty-four hours later and Sonia was flown south, with Sarah, to the naval air station at Yeovilton in Somerset. Nairn ordered her to be received with courtesy and driven to Edge twenty-five miles away. Still astonished at the turn of events, he needed time to adjust to the knowledge that Sonia, despite all the odds, was actually back on British soil. Cornered at last.

191

It was barely eight in the morning when they reached the country house, for they had been taken to the airfield outside Glasgow straight from the submarine base after docking at five a.m. The housekeeper opened the heavy oak door as the two cars crunched round the gravel circle. The first car held four armed police in uniform, the second Sonia, Sarah, a driver and two men from the department, also armed. A stand-off car was following a mile behind. The police got out and turned to face the rhododendron bushes with drawn revolvers, looking faintly absurd.

Sarah opened the rear door of the dark blue Rover and Sonia followed her into the hall, their footsteps hollow on the flagstones. The old woman stumbled and the girl grabbed her arm, feeling the shrivelled skin loose on Sonia's wrist and thin bones frail between her fingers. 'You must be exhausted,' she said. 'This is a place to rest. They've prepared a sitting room and a bedroom for you – I do hope you'll be comfortable. Would you like to sleep straightaway?'

Sonia nodded, her eyes opaque with fear and confusion. 'Am I a prisoner?'

'Oh, I wouldn't say that. You can't leave here, but I promise we'll treat you honourably. Someone senior to me will be here to talk to you when you wake up.'

As soon as Sonia was asleep, Sarah checked that the two armed guards were staying on duty in the house and the police inspector told her that he had been instructed to provide four constables with revolvers to patrol outside for the next twenty-four hours. Satisfied, Sarah was driven on towards London. As the Rover crossed the green expanse of Salisbury Plain and sped up the M3, she wondered whether she would ever be allowed to see the courageous old woman again.

The car left the M3 at Staines and Nairn was waiting at a clapboard bungalow by the river in Shepperton. He met her in the porch, took her in his arms and kissed her. 'Thank God you're safe, Sarah, and well done. *Very* well done. You were tremendous, a real pro.'

She started to cry with relief as Nairn hugged her like a father. He led her into a shabby sitting room and they sat on a sofa. She wept happily into his shoulder. 'Oh, David, I've been so scared. It was *terrifying*. Thank you for getting me out.'

'I should never have let you go in.'

'You didn't, it was my decision – and a mistake. I must have been mad.' She looked up, blinking through her tears. 'And I *wasn't* tremendous – I was bloody awful. I had no business to go waltzing off into East Berlin and I nearly got Sonia killed and wrecked everything.' He did not dissent but hugged her again, eyes unreadable below the bushy eyebrows. 'Whose house is this?' she asked.

'The department's. We've had it since the war; it's convenient for Heathrow airport.' He stroked her face gently. 'Now tell me, what actually happened up there in the Baltic?'

'An East German coastguard cutter shot us up and two of the SBS men were killed.' She started to weep again, sobbing but reassured by his arms. 'I've never seen anybody killed before. I fell in the sea and the third man – Sergeant Evans – pulled me out. God knows how, he was pouring blood from a wound in his neck. Somehow he bundled me down a hatch on the submarine's deck just before it dived. Sonia came down seconds later. I'd lost sight of her in the chaos, but he must have fished her out of the water too.'

'And Evans managed to escape himself?'

'Oh yes, I couldn't forgive myself if he'd died after saving me. Then he collapsed – he must have lost a hell of a lot of blood, I was soaked in it. The other two men were washed away.'

Nairn nodded. 'Poor bastards . . . what happened after that?'

'Sonia was very shocked and they put her in a little cabin to sleep. I felt hysterical and very sick – I'd swallowed gallons of salt water – but after howling for a bit I calmed down and got cleaned up. They gave me some sailor's clothes and I just sat in a corner until we surfaced in the North Sea. I sat in one place so long I'll have the rivet marks on my backside permanently.' She giggled, then started to cry again. 'It was very hot, I can't remember much else.'

Nairn smiled distantly. 'Try to go back forty-eight hours,

if you can. Do you think they were expecting you in East Berlin?'

'Oh yes, they were expecting me, David. At least, they were expecting *someone*. I was blown from the start, no doubt about that.'

'I was afraid so, but I had no inkling of it before you went in. I learnt something just a few days ago . . . I'm sorry.'

'It doesn't matter now, but it wasn't *just* that they were waiting for me.' She frowned. 'At the end – on the beach, I think – I began to mistrust Sonia. I felt sorry for her in Berlin, but later there was something wrong.'

'What exactly?'

'She was playing a part, as if she expected us to be stopped before we left the country.'

'Perhaps.'

'She was very shocked to find herself actually on the submarine.'

'I bet she was. But you were alone with her for several hours – did she say anything of interest?'

'Oh yes, I was saving that up.' Sarah grinned at him triumphantly. 'I got what you wanted, David. Sonia was in a very emotional state on the beach and became quite talkative. In the end she broke down and told me the name of the traitor.'

'*Did* she now?' Nairn looked less surprised than she had expected. 'And whom did she name?'

Sarah stared at him quizzically. For a moment she wondered if he had made her love him to engineer all that had happened – but no, that was too fanciful. 'Carteret. Sonia said it was Carteret. She was quite emphatic.' She smiled as Nairn kissed her. 'Of course, it's what we thought all the time, but at least you can be sure now.'

He nodded thoughtfully. 'Did she say anything else?'

'She seemed a bit surprised that we wanted so much to know. She said his real importance had been in the last war. He went on afterwards, but was ambivalent and only produced anything useful at rare intervals.'

'And did you believe her?'

'Yes, I did. But I see what you mean . . . now I'm not sure.'

194

He shook his head, staring through the grimy window, across the overgrown garden, to the grey waters of the Thames. 'Whoever else it may have been, it wasn't Carteret. What you've just been through is the culmination of twenty years work to convince us that he was the traitor. They want us to believe that *very* much, to incriminate an innocent man to conceal their real penetration, and, if we keep our heads down, with a bit of luck they'll think we were taken in.'

As he turned back into the room, she met his gaze ruefully, grey eyes large in a face that was suddenly young and troubled. 'I made an awful mess of it, didn't I?'

'No, of course not. You were being manipulated by the most devious mind in the business.'

'That's kind of you, David, but I still think I'd better find something else to do – I'm not up to all this. I always meant to go to university after a year or so at Century – maybe I should do that now, go and sort myself out. I'm only twenty-two.'

Nairn put his arm round her shoulders and they walked out on to the towpath. 'Maybe you should – but not because you're a failure, Sarah. This time you brought back exactly what I wanted.' Again she felt a cold knot inside, as if reacting against being used like a pawn on his chessboard. He wasn't naturally manipulative but the job made it inevitable. Sarah could see that side more clearly now – and it was frightening. He was kind and maddeningly attractive, but no woman could love him for long unless she knew and cared nothing for the service.

He was smiling at her. 'We'll talk about it later. You've had a rough time and you're feeling shocked, so don't rush into anything.' The deep-set eyes searched hers. 'As a matter of fact, I know a tutor at Oxford who might like to talk to you, if you're interested.'

'Just now it's all too much – what I'd really like is a bath.'

'Surely, even this dump has a bathroom and hot water – and they fetched some of your own clothes from your flat in Clapham. There's a case in the bedroom. Then shall we go somewhere cosy for lunch?'

'That would be lovely, but is there time? You've got Sonia – and everything else – to sort out, haven't you?'

195

'She's safe at Edge. I don't think she'll expire on us if she's survived this far and the Carteret case has lasted twenty years; it can wait a little longer. I'm meeting Simon and Alexander at four this afternoon – in the meantime we're going to the City Barge, where I first recruited you, remember?'

There was an awkward silence until Alexander looked searchingly at Nairn. 'And if it wasn't Carteret, who the blazes was it?'

'It has to be Fell,' interrupted Simon. 'And I want the bastard brought in for interrogation straightaway. They *must* have been protecting Fell – and whoever he left behind him.' He glared at Nairn, who remained impassive. 'Of course David, bless his cotton socks, disagrees. Well,' he snapped accusingly. 'Don't you?'

Nairn leaned back in his chair, thinking of the three graveyards he'd visited on this bloody case. Each by a typically English church with a fine stone tower, set in a tiny backwater of a village: St Peter's on the Somerset Levels, St Andrew's in the Chilterns, St Laud's on the flat plains of Buckinghamshire. It was hard to imagine either of the old men who had retired to those dull, unpicturesque backwaters as a traitor, yet Sonia had lived in Great Rollright for five years and buried her parents there – and there was no doubt about *her* . . .

'It wasn't Carteret,' he said slowly. 'It *could* have been Fell, but I don't see enough evidence to be sure. It's quite possible they were both innocent. Certainly there was someone betraying Five back in the war, when Sonia was courier for Fuchs – that was what really mattered, building the bomb. She bust the nuclear programme and someone shielded her so we let her go. Whoever it was would probably have gone on after the war, but he could have died years ago. Often I'm inclined to believe he did.'

'Well, *I* don't. It's absurd to suggest the whole Carteret/Fell thing was disinformation,' snapped Simon. 'Good God, man, just think of all the work that's gone into the investigation, years and years of it. One of them *has* to be a spy.'

'*Somebody* certainly was,' said Nairn quietly. 'But the last twenty years could simply have been the Centre feeding our suspicion with snippets of evidence, a long complicated false trail.'

'What the hell for?'

'To destroy Five, to wreck all confidence in it in Whitehall and Westminster, while outside their stooges attack it for infringing civil liberties. To destroy its credibility – not a bad ploy if subversion's your aim. Wreck something by playing on its built-in weaknesses; we've had so many moles we see them at every corner now, even when they don't exist.'

Alexander's parchment cheeks quivered angrily. 'That's balls, Nairn, absolute balls. I agree about Carteret – the Sonia episode proves it – so that leaves Fell. The bloody man's been drawing his pension from the Queen all these years after a lifetime of working for Moscow. It's sickening. He'll be picked up at dawn tomorrow, not invited back like an honoured guest as he was before, and put under hostile interrogation. We'll get the truth – and if he left a successor, by all that's holy we'll have him or her too.'

'I entirely agree.' Simon closed the file in front of him. 'And you, David, will arrange for Sonia to be brought up from Edge tomorrow morning.'

'By helicopter?'

'One of your department's cars will do. Provide an armed escort, we don't want to lose her. She must be questioned thoroughly. Respect her age, but don't be too kid-gloved. She can't go back to the East and she's still liable to trial for treason here. No real question of that, of course, but you've got some strong levers to make her co-operate.'

'And then?'

'When we are ready, we confront them with each other. My God, that should be a shock after thirty-five years – that will clinch it.'

Nairn nodded. 'I'll do what you say, but I don't like it and I don't believe it will work.'

'Just *do* it, Nairn,' coughed Alexander, rheumy eyes furious in their deep sockets. 'Get the bloody woman up here and I'll see to Fell. After that,' he sneered, 'if you've no stomach for it, I'm sure Simon and I can manage without you.'

41

London

At six the next morning, two cars sped up the M1 from Hendon, both anonymous blue Ford Cortinas containing three men. Even to Alexander, who had briefed them personally at his office in Curzon Street, it seemed a large group to invite a man of nearly eighty to return for a talk with his old employers. The cars left the motorway at Newport Pagnell, taking a side road that wound across the dull, flat fields of the Buckingham–Bedford borderland.

The village was still asleep, for it was Saturday, and no one observed the first car as it parked in a cul-de-sac leading to the church. The back garden wall of the bungalow gave on to the cul-de-sac and the three men spread out along it, one fingering the revolver in his belt. The second car parked in a lane near the White Hart Inn and two other men approached the entrance to the little close of modern houses and bungalows.

In London, Nairn started the day with a solitary walk along the towpath. He had woken early, after a restless night, and drawn his curtains to see the sun rise over the jumbled roofs of Chiswick. Twenty minutes later he had passed the City Barge and was leaning on a railing watching two sleeping swans, heads tucked into their feathers. He stayed there, lost in thought, for nearly an hour.

Sarah was a remarkable girl, mature for her age and, thank God, no worse for her experience. Who knows, she might be back in three years . . . As for Five, they could keep it. And plainly they were going to. He'd stay on at Century for another year if Walker would let him, but he wasn't going to die in harness like Alexander. It had been a daft idea of Jim Simon's anyway. He looked at his watch as he approached Kew Bridge. It was nearly nine o'clock, about the right time for the phone call he was steeling himself to make. He turned and hurried back to the flat. The telephone was ringing when he opened the door.

The two men approached the front door of the bungalow in the half-light at seven o'clock. One knocked with the brass lion's-head knocker, but there was no answer. He knocked again, harder, and bedroom curtains in the other houses were drawn aside nosily at the racket. A red post office van drove into the close and parked. The grey-uniformed postman got out and started to deliver letters as if nothing unusual were happening; after progressing steadily up and down three other garden paths he opened the gate behind them.

"Morning. You looking for Mr Fell, then?'

The taller man, absurd in trench-coat and bowler hat, turned round. 'Yes, we are.'

'Sorry mate, you're too late. He died of a heart attack yesterday; and she's gone away – to her daughter's I think. Very nice bloke, too.'

As the postman turned away the two men looked at each other. 'Oh Christ,' muttered trench-coat. 'We'd better verify – ring the local hospital, I suppose?'

His companion nodded. 'The DG isn't going to like this, you know. He'll go berserk – they'll never know the truth now, not a hundred per cent. Just twenty-four hours too late. What a fuck-up.'

Sarah had been clearing her desk in Century House when the muddled phone call came through from Somerset and Avon Constabulary. The switchboard were uncertain how to handle it and the fact that they tried Nairn's special section was accidental.

After ringing Nairn at the flat in Chiswick, she ignored his instructions to go home. She was leaving the service anyway, so why the hell shouldn't she see the case, *her* case, through to the end? Her car was in the basement car park and it took her just over two hours to speed down the motorway to the scene of the accident. She turned south at

Bristol, reflecting that she was passing the city where Klaus Fuchs had come as a refugee and, twenty minutes later, the village where Carteret had died.

The car was in a lane north of Taunton. It was burnt out, metal body twisted and blackened. Brown gashes in the grass showed where it had skidded off the road to smash into a stone wall. Nearby were two police cars, blue lights flashing, and half a dozen constables standing about aimlessly. One of them tried to wave Sarah on, but she pulled the MG sideways, wheels bouncing on the verge, and stopped. As she scrambled out a police sergeant ran up, gesturing her to get back in the car.

'I'm from the Foreign Office,' she said firmly. 'Defence Department. They sent me to report as soon as we heard about the accident.'

The sergeant looked suspicious. 'Press, are you?'

'No. Foreign Office.'

'Do you have something to prove your identity?' He spoke in a thick Somerset burr.

'No, I don't. We don't carry ID cards.'

'Not a funny, are you? Look – I'll have to check.'

'Yes, do that,' she smiled briskly. 'Now, where are the bodies?'

'Bodies? What bodies? This is a traffic accident. You just wait in the car like a good girl.'

Sarah took a step forward. 'I'm not your good girl, I'm here on urgent business. So for Christ's sake go and get permission to talk to me – I haven't got time to piss about all day!'

The sergeant's face darkened – he was not used to being shouted at by elegant young blondes in MGs – but he shambled off to his car. 'Spanking's what you need,' he muttered under his breath.

'What was that, Sergeant?'

'I said the bodies were taken to the mortuary in Taunton, Miss.'

'How many of them?'

'Four, Miss.'

Sarah nodded curtly and walked over to the smoking car. Two of the four tyres had burst, shreds of rubber clinging to the twisted metal of the wheels. The doors hung open and the interior was a mass of soot-blackened springs and PVC. Gingerly she put her head inside, but any trace of blood had been obliterated by the fire.

She went back to the sergeant, who was leaning into a police car, talking slowly into a microphone. He looked up questioningly, but no longer aggressive, almost respectful. 'Can I help you, Miss?'

'I'll need to use a secure telephone – I expect your Special Branch have one?'

Nairn arrived by helicopter in a field near Taunton an hour and a half later; the Westland Lynx with naval markings had picked him up from a school playing field close to his flat in Chiswick. Sarah met him and they drove back into town in her MG with an escort of two police cars. No more cars containing SIS officers were to be allowed to crash in flames on the territory of the Somerset and Avon Constabulary.

'Where to?' she asked briskly. 'The mortuary?'

Nairn grunted an affirmative.

'They say they're burnt beyond recognition, but I suppose you should see for yourself.'

He grunted again.

'Oh for God's sake,' she screamed. 'Don't just sit there – *say* something. Damn you, David, we've worked and slaved for weeks and I've risked my life to get that bloody woman to defect and now she's *dead*. We've been waiting *forty years* for this. All that effort, all that risk, it's so sickening I'd be kicking and weeping if I wasn't driving the man who's just failed to become head of MI5.' She beat her hands on the steering wheel.

'Please don't kill us,' said Nairn laconically.

'Why the bloody hell not? Oh, David, you berk. You stupid, stupid berk! You're the best of them all, but you've really cocked it up this time. What the hell were you *doing* letting her be ferried about in an ordinary car like that?'

'There were three guards, all armed.'

'For Christ's sake, they move bloody banknotes in bullet-proof vans with radio contact. You had the most valuable defector ever, but no police escort, no radio, just a few blokes with toy guns who drive off the road and bloody kill her. It's pathetic! Oh, David, I'm so angry . . .'

'Ay – I had that impression.' Sarah was parking outside a modern hospital and the police cars were edging in beside her. They followed a policeman into a side door, down a corridor with pipes running along the ceiling, and out into a yard. The mortuary was a small building set apart from the rest of the hospital. The policeman pushed open a sliding door and they entered a long, white-painted chamber. One wall consisted of a row of doors, each about five feet high and painted with three numbers to mark the steel trays within. There was a faint whirr from cooling fans.

Another constable was standing guard. 'This is Sir David Nairn,' said their guide. 'Can you call Dr Rathbone?' He turned to Nairn. 'Rathbone's the pathologist.' They waited awkwardly for ten minutes until the doctor appeared. He was an angular, breathless man with a look of permanent irritation. 'We usually lay bodies out in the chapel for identification, but you're not exactly relatives, are you?'

'No. We don't want to put you to any trouble,' said Nairn.

'You already have – I'm supposed to be off duty.' The pathologist nodded curtly to a white-coated technician, who opened one of the low doors. Freezing air flooded out. A bulkhead light showed three bodies inside the refrigerator, each in a greenish-grey polythene bag.

'Which one do you want to see first?' asked the pathologist abruptly. 'There are two unidentified males in here and one female.'

'The woman, please.'

The technician drew out one of the galvanized trays, rattling on steel rollers. 'It's not a pretty sight, sir.' He spoke apologetically, with a soft West Country accent.

The pathologist leaned forward and unzipped the body bag to reveal a charred head and upper torso. Sarah winced as she saw the blackened skin, fused with strips of burnt clothing and flaky like charcoal. The post mortem incision had been sewn up in a wavy line down the chest. The pungent, sickly-sweet smell made her want to vomit.

'Burns smell worse than ordinary corpses,' explained the doctor, pointing with a chromium instrument to where half

202

the face was missing. 'But these are unusual for an RTA.'

'For a what?' queried Nairn.

'Road traffic accident. Flesh doesn't burn well, not even in petrol, but all these bodies are very badly damaged.'

'What was the cause of death?'

'Bullet wounds to head and chest in three cases.'

'They were *shot*?' Sarah met Nairn's eyes in shared horror.

'Certainly – didn't the police tell you? How odd. I did the autopsies this afternoon. So many lesions that they must have been dead before the fire. The woman wasn't shot in the head but in the back by a dozen high velocity bullets, so she couldn't have been sitting in the car at the time.'

'In the back?' Sarah flinched as the body bag was opened further and she saw the twisted metal of the Chinese ring on the left hand, blackened but unmistakable.

'We always leave rings on,' said the technician.

'Oh my God,' breathed Sarah, leaning forward despite the vile smell to see the remains of the face.

42

Taunton

The car was travelling at about sixty when the first bullets raked its wheels. Both the nearside tyres burst and it skidded off the road with a shriek of metal, tearing up the verge and smashing into the stone wall with a spine-jarring crash.

A man sprinted from a gateway, crouching low and holding a smoking Heckler and Koch machine pistol; another appeared from behind the wall, similarly armed. They approached the car cautiously, both in black boiler suits, but there was no sign of movement. The blue bonnet was crumpled and lacerated by flying fragments of flint, the windscreen opaque with crazed glass. In the front two figures were slumped motionless over the dashboard.

One rear door was locked from the inside but the other had burst open. They pulled it back warily and covered the three figures on the back seat, all of whom were conscious but dazed. The man nearest to them raised a revolver defensively, but before he could speak a stream of bullets hammered into his chest. He rolled out of the car and collapsed in a pool of blood. The other guard tried to fend them off as they pulled the woman through the door, but a gun butt smashed into his face and he reeled back with a scream, clutching at his eyes, crimson seeping between his fingers.

The taller man helped Sonia to stagger from the wreckage. 'Quickly – we have come to rescue you,' he said in Russian. His companion fired a short burst at the screaming guard in the back of the Rover, then a single shot into the head of the unconscious driver in the front. Sonia averted her eyes from the carnage and leant on the man's arm.

'Just finish it,' she muttered. 'There was no need for all this.'

'They were concerned that you should not be interrogated, Colonel.' He leered as he emphasized her military rank, leading her towards a gateway, where he paused and glared at her anxiously. '*Have* you been questioned yet, Colonel?'

'No.'

'Not at all?'

'No, not at all.' She spoke irritably and felt his arm withdraw. He stepped back sharply. She half turned in surprise as he raised the machine pistol, pitching forward when the bullets shattered her spine.

There was an uncanny silence after the shooting. Within seconds the bodies of Sonia and the guard had been replaced on the back seat of the car, Sonia wedged between the two dead men. The traces of her blood were wiped up from the tarmac with a piece of rag. Both men stripped off their overalls, to reveal neat business suits, and hurled them into the car, followed by a plastic container of a brown solvent. When the hired Datsun was out of the gateway, facing the motorway with its engine running, the taller man turned and fired three rapid shots into the rear of the Rover, where he estimated its petrol tank ought to be. There was a thin crackle of yellow flame, which spread hesitantly until suddenly the whole vehicle was a roaring mass of orange fire.

It was less than two minutes since their first bullets had struck the car; in another five they were on the M5, anonymous in the traffic heading north for Bristol. Before a patrolling police car found the wreckage, they had reached Bristol airport and checked in on Aer Lingus flight EI 283 to Dublin. One had a West German passport, the other travelled on Danish documents; but before the day was out they would be bound for Sofia, both using passports issued by their own government.

'Poor, poor Sonia.' Nairn's voice was barely a whisper. 'They betrayed her when they took Sorge from Shanghai; and again when they kept his execution from her. Now the third and last betrayal . . .'

'What did you say?' snapped the pathologist.

205

Sarah intervened. 'Could you identify the bullets?'

'I'm not a ballistics expert – the police have taken them away to forensic – but . . .'

'Yes?'

'Well, I *have* seen bullets before – we get our fair share of murder and suicide here – so I'm familiar with those in common use. But these people were killed by ammunition I'd never seen before – and the cartridge cases the police picked up and chucked in the body bags had foreign markings.'

'Yes – that's what I'd expect.'

'Have they found the people who did it?'

'Not yet.'

The pathologist looked at Nairn curiously. 'Can't imagine why not. I'd have thought it would be easy. A couple of thugs shoot up four people in broad daylight only a few miles from a big town – where the devil can they go?'

'I'm sure the police will find them soon.'

'I damn well hope so. Can't think what this bloody country's coming to.'

Back in the car park it had started to rain. Sarah clutched at Nairn's arm as they walked slowly to the car. 'She didn't deserve that,' she cried out. 'It's all a myth about the Centre looking after their own. She was sixty years in the Party, a heroine, yet they silenced her in case she talked. Oh David, it's so *squalid*.'

'I think we may find they silenced Fell too. I thought it was just a heart attack, a piece of monumentally bad timing, but not after this.'

Sarah started and stared at him. 'Is *Fell* dead as well?'

'Yesterday evening. His doctor certified a heart attack.'

'Don't they have little gas guns that cause choking and heart failure, so it looks like a natural death.'

Nairn nodded unhappily. 'Yes, they've had them for years. It could easily have been done. A caller late last night at the bungalow when his wife was out, perhaps a familiar face from the Soviet Embassy, a friendly word, a whiff of gas in the face – I forget what it is, probably cyanide – and he'd be gone. Undetectable.'

'And no one can ever question either of them now. If Fell left a successor, even a whole *line* of successors . . .' She started the car, clinging to the steering wheel because her hands were trembling.

'I don't believe he did,' said Nairn firmly. 'I just don't believe he did.'

It was not until late in the evening, when he was alone in Chiswick, that the nagging doubt finally surfaced. The long deception was over, Kirov had failed and it was a time for two cheers; he poured himself a single malt in a solitary victory celebration. Fell – elusive, brave, lonely, treacherous Fell – was the key. If he had not worked alone, if there *were* still someone in the system, now they understood what they were looking for . . .

And then he knew. The elimination of Sonia had been too quick, too clean; somehow the hit men must have known she was travelling – every last detail of the route. The more he tried to push the knowledge away, the more certain he became; and suddenly the mellow golden liquid, with its slight tang of peat, tasted like acid in his mouth.

The Sealink ferry from Portsmouth steamed into Cherbourg at seven on Sunday morning, past the derelict sheds of the old ocean liner terminal. The young couple turned from the rail, where they had watched a misty horizon turn into the green coastline of Normandy, the man stooping to pick up their child. 'Daddy,' she pointed to the bent figure still gazing out to sea as he had for the past hour. 'Why does the old man look so sad?' But the question was lost in the chatter from the companionway down to the car deck.

The elderly man had no car and no luggage. He wore a shabby overcoat and old felt hat, waiting conspicuously among the red and yellow anoraks of hitchhikers and cyclists as the gangway rose from the quay. Hurrying across the cobbles to the queue through immigration, he flinched as the two men in dark suits appeared at his sides.

'Your passport, please, m'sieur.' The policeman's eyes scanned the dark blue document and met the old man's gaze with contempt. 'No, m'sieur, you are not Mr Pritchard. I have reason to believe that you are Sir James Simon and I have been asked by the British authorities to detain you.'

*

When Nairn reached Great Rollright late on Sunday afternoon she was waiting for him in the kitchen. 'Why wouldn't you meet me in Oxford?' she asked, eyes and auburn hair shining under the bare bulb hanging from the beams. 'It would have saved you driving out to this dump.'

'I wanted to come here again, to see where my spy lived.'

'When you rang last night, I thought for a minute you might be coming to see *me*.' She gave a broad *gamine* grin before he could reply. 'Don't look so serious, David Nairn.'

'Sorry.' He smiled at her, but she met his eyes quizzically. 'There's something wrong, isn't there?'

'Nothing important.'

'You've changed since you phoned me.' She took his hand. 'It was very sad about that man Simon, the refugee who turned out to be a spy. I heard it on the radio – such a rotten way to go, hanging yourself in a foreign police cell.'

Nairn hesitated. 'I worked with him, Alison.'

'I guessed you did.' She drew him to her as if she had known him for years; her touch was gentle and seemed to convey some of her vitality and warmth. 'I'm sorry – he must have been very lonely at the end. It must be awful for you too – did you know him very well?'

'We worked together for twenty years. I thought he was a friend.'

'Do you think it's true, then, that he was already a communist when he came here from Vienna all those years ago, when he was only nineteen?'

'I just don't know – if so, he concealed it uncommonly well.'

'Can you talk about it?'

'No. Not today. Probably never. I shouldn't have said anything. Anyway, I came to take you out, not to whinge about my problems.' She saw the defensive, troubled look in his eyes and did not press. Abruptly he changed the subject. 'The house is very quiet – what's happened to all the children?'

'They don't stay for long, just a few weeks when a crisis blows up. They've all gone except my two teenagers – and they're out for the day. I haven't decided whether to take any more – maybe I've recovered enough to do something else now.'

'What would you like to do?'

'For life or for the evening?'

'Let's work out the evening first.'

'You choose. I can't take decisions.' She stood up with a laugh and kissed him on the forehead. 'Actually I was wrong – you're not terrifying at all – and if you don't feel like being macho and decisive, I'd like to go to a pub I know in Oxford. It's full of students, throbbing with life. After that it's up to you.' She looked away shyly. 'Don't look so troubled, I feel a bit odd, too – I haven't been out with a stranger since Tom died.'

He smiled. 'Then I'm very honoured.'

'Yes, you are.' She gave a ribald chuckle and the tension had gone as he took her in his arms and kissed her; they walked out into the yard hand in hand, their feet crunching on the gravel. She left the kitchen door open and turned back as Nairn paused to close it. 'Thanks, I always forget to do that.' She smiled serenely as he put his arm round her waist, and snuggled into his shoulder. 'You know, David, I don't know *anything* about you.'

'There's not much to know.'

'I don't believe that. By the way,' she turned and looked at him thoughtfully. 'Did you find what you were looking for?'

'How do you mean?'

'When you were here last time you were looking for something, weren't you? I wondered whether you found it, that's all.'

At the car he opened the door and smiled at her. 'Yes, I think perhaps I did.'

Postscript

The Third Betrayal is a work of fiction and is not intended to be read as anything else.

The characters are all fictitious, with the exception of Richard Sorge, who was a leading agent of the Fourth Bureau of the Red Army (now GRU, Soviet Military Intelligence) in the Far East from 1929–44. After serving in China, he infiltrated the German Embassy in Tokyo in the years before the Second World War. Posing as a German journalist and a Nazi, he became one of the most important spies of the war. Through him, Moscow knew that Japan did not intend to invade Russia from the East and was therefore able to throw all her force against the German invasion from the West. Even then, Stalin came close to defeat. Sorge was captured by the Japanese and hanged in 1944.

Ruth Kuczynski was also a courageous and skilful intelligence officer, whose association with Richard Sorge appears to have changed the course of her life. It seemed pointless, and a little disrespectful, to give other names to characters based on two such distinguished and self-confessed Soviet agents. However, the character of Sonia in the book, though inspired by Ruth Kuczynski, should be seen as entirely fictitious. At certain points, Ruth Kuczynski's memoirs of her years as a spy, published in the German Democratic Republic in 1977, have been drawn upon and at these points the plot may come close to reality; but Kuczynski herself has implied that her memoirs may not be entirely accurate, writing in them that 'every author has difficulty in the writing of memoirs: selecting, compromising and telling the truth, that was my way.' Otherwise, her character, actions and the events she lives through in *The Third Betrayal* are fictional – and, from the Second World War onwards, completely imaginary. The real Ruth Kuczynski has not defected to the

West and, so far as is known, is still alive in honoured retirement in East Germany.

The other characters also are all fictitious and, to emphasize this, with the exception of Len Beurton's and the forenames of Sonia's children, no other real names are used. According to her memoirs, Ruth Kuczynski's first husband was an architect from Berlin, but his name was not Friedmann. According to the same source, her second husband, Len Beurton, was British and her three children had the forenames used, but neither Len nor her three children are intended to be portrayed personally in the book. So far as is known, none of them uses the surname Werner and nor does Ruth Kuczynski, although she has used it as a pen-name.

Similarly, all events in the book should be seen as fictitious. Like many thrillers, *The Third Betrayal* is inspired by real-life Soviet espionage activity, but if it trespasses on truth at any point, that is entirely coincidental.

SEVEN STEPS TO TREASON

'Off to a racing start . . . a dignified thriller.'
Observer

'Devilishly clever – by an author on his way to the élite in his genre.'
Manchester Evening News

'Brilliant tale of espionage . . . a new master thriller writer.'
Western Morning News

'A stunning display of diplomatic and undercover know-how, of SAS dare-devilry and global double-cross'
Sunday Times

Adventure Thriller 0 7221 4201 3
£2.50

DOWN AMONG THE DEAD MEN

'Cleverly plotted and impressive.'

Guardian

'Superbly captured exotic Far East backgrounds and an array of spooks who seem very real indeed . . . a cracking debut.'

Yorkshire Post

'Thwacking Far East spy story.'

H. R. F. Keating

'A dazzling first novel . . . Hartland joins le Carré and Len Deighton as a master-hand'

Best Sellers

Adventure Thriller 0 7221 4196 3
£1.95

A top secret SBS mission during the Falklands
War soars into explosive action . . .

SPECIAL DELIVERANCE

ALEXANDER FULLERTON

In the war-torn, storm-swept South Atlantic, a small band of
highly-trained SBS experts embark on a vital secret mission: to
sabotage Argentina's stock of deadly Exocet missiles.

The dangers are unthinkable: the coastline is exposed and treacherous,
the missile base is surrounded by vast tracts of open land, they must
infiltrate and destroy without ever being detected. Some say it's
impossible . . . but no one underestimates the SBS's lethal capacity.

And one man, Andy MacEwan, an Anglo-Argentine civilian recruited to
the team as guide and interpreter, has more than the success of the
mission on his mind. His brother is a commander in the Argentine Navy
Air Force and there is no love lost between them . . .

*'Good rollicking stuff – full of tension and highly authentic on SBS
technique'*
TODAY

'The action passages are superb. He is in a class of his own'
OBSERVER

0 7221 3719 2   ADVENTURE THRILLER   £2.99

THE HYPNOTIC POWER OF SOUL-CHILLING
TERROR . . .

Death Trance

Graham
Masterton

Respectable businessman Randolph Clare, president of one
of Tennessee's largest companies, is challenging the
bureaucratic Cottonseed Association with lower prices and
greater efficiency. But then tragedy strikes – his wife and
children are savagely and brutally murdered . . .

In desperation Randolph makes contact with an Indonesian
priest who claims he can help him enter the world of the
dead. But there demons await, hungry for those who dare
make the journey. Not only do they want Randolph's life,
but are eager to condemn his family's souls to a hell of agony
far beyond all human imagination . . .

Don't miss Graham Masterton's other horror classics:
REVENGE OF THE MANITOU   THE WELLS OF HELL
THE DEVILS OF D-DAY   THE HEIRLOOM
CHARNEL HOUSE   TENGU
NIGHT WARRIORS

0 7221 6124 7   HORROR   £2.99

A selection of bestsellers from Sphere

FICTION

WHITE SUN, RED STAR	Robert Elegant	£3.50 ☐
A TASTE FOR DEATH	P. D. James	£3.50 ☐
THE PRINCESS OF POOR STREET	Emma Blair	£2.99 ☐
WANDERLUST	Danielle Steel	£3.50 ☐
LADY OF HAY	Barbara Erskine	£3.95 ☐

FILM AND TV TIE-IN

BLACK FOREST CLINIC	Peter Heim	£2.99 ☐
INTIMATE CONTACT	Jacqueline Osborne	£2.50 ☐
BEST OF BRITISH	Maurice Sellar	£8.95 ☐
SEX WITH PAULA YATES	Paula Yates	£2.95 ☐
RAW DEAL	Walter Wager	£2.50 ☐

NON-FICTION

INVISIBLE ARMIES	Stephen Segaller	£4.99 ☐
ALEX THROUGH THE LOOKING GLASS	Alex Higgins with Tony Francis	£2.99 ☐
NEXT TO A LETTER FROM HOME: THE GLENN MILLER STORY	Geoffrey Butcher	£4.99 ☐
AS TIME GOES BY: THE LIFE OF INGRID BERGMAN	Laurence Leamer	£3.95 ☐
BOTHAM	Don Mosey	£3.50 ☐

All Sphere books are available at your local bookshop or newsagent, or can be ordered direct from the publisher. Just tick the titles you want and fill in the form below.

Name _____

Address _____

_____

Write to Sphere Books, Cash Sales Department, P.O. Box 11, Falmouth, Cornwall TR10 9EN

Please enclose a cheque or postal order to the value of the cover price plus:

UK: 60p for the first book, 25p for the second book and 15p for each additional book ordered to a maximum charge of £1.90.

OVERSEAS & EIRE: £1.25 for the first book, 75p for the second book and 28p for each subsequent title ordered.

BFPO: 60p for the first book, 25p for the second book plus 15p per copy for the next 7 books, thereafter 9p per book.

Sphere Books reserve the right to show new retail prices on covers which may differ from those previously advertised in the text elsewhere, and to increase postal rates in accordance with the P.O.